Some Short Stories

Henry James

Kessinger Publishing reprints thousands of hard–to–find books!

Visit us at http://www.kessinger.net

BROOKSMITH

We are scattered now, the friends of the late Mr. Oliver Offord; but whenever we chance to meet I think we are conscious of a certain esoteric respect for each other. "Yes, you too have been in Arcadia," we seem not too grumpily to allow. When I pass the house in Mansfield Street I remember that Arcadia was there. I don't know who has it now, and don't want to know; it's enough to be so sure that if I should ring the bell there would be no such luck for me as that Brooksmith should open the door. Mr. Offord, the most agreeable, the most attaching of bachelors, was a retired diplomatist, living on his pension and on something of his own over and above; a good deal confined, by his infirmities, to his fireside and delighted to be found there any afternoon in the year, from five o'clock on, by such visitors as Brooksmith allowed to come up. Brooksmith was his butler and his most intimate friend, to whom we all stood, or I should say sat, in the same relation in which the subject of the sovereign finds himself to the prime minister. By having been for years, in foreign lands, the most delightful Englishman any one had ever known, Mr. Offord had in my opinion rendered signal service to his country. But I suppose he had been too much liked—liked even by those who didn't like IT—so that as people of that sort never get titles or dotations for the horrid things they've NOT done, his principal reward was simply that we went to see him.

Oh we went perpetually, and it was not our fault if he was not overwhelmed with this particular honour. Any visitor who came once came again; to come merely once was a slight nobody, I'm sure, had ever put upon him. His circle therefore was essentially composed of habitues, who were habitues for each other as well as for him, as those of a happy salon should be. I remember vividly every element of the place, down to the intensely Londonish look of the grey opposite houses, in the gap of the white curtains of the high windows, and the exact spot where, on a particular afternoon, I put down my tea–cup for Brooksmith, lingering an instant, to gather it up as if he were plucking a flower. Mr. Offord's drawing–room was indeed Brooksmith's garden, his pruned and tended human parterre, and if we all flourished there and grew well in our places it was largely owing to his supervision.

Many persons have heard much, though most have doubtless seen little, of the famous institution of the salon, and many are born to the depression of knowing that this finest flower of social life refuses to bloom where the English tongue is spoken. The explanation is usually that our women have not the skill to cultivate it—the art to direct through a smiling land, between suggestive shores, a sinuous stream of talk. My affectionate, my pious memory of Mr. Offord contradicts this induction only, I fear, more insidiously to confirm it. The sallow and slightly smoked drawing–room in which he spent so large a portion of the last years of his life certainly deserved the distinguished name; but on the other hand it couldn't be said at all to owe its stamp to any intervention throwing into relief the fact that there was no Mrs. Offord. The dear man had indeed, at the most, been capable of one of those sacrifices to which women are deemed peculiarly apt: he had recognised—under the influence, in some degree, it is true, of physical infirmity—that if you wish people to find you at home you must manage not to be out. He had in short accepted the truth which many dabblers in the social art are slow to learn, that you must really, as they say, take a line, and that the only way as yet discovered of being at home is to stay at home. Finally his own fireside had become a summary of his habits. Why should he ever have left it?—since this would have been leaving what was notoriously pleasantest in London, the compact charmed cluster (thinning away indeed into casual couples) round the fine old last– century chimney–piece which, with the exception of the remarkable collection of miniatures, was the best thing the place contained. Mr. Offord wasn't rich; he had nothing but his pension and the use for life of the somewhat superannuated house.

When I'm reminded by some opposed discomfort of the present hour how perfectly we were all handled there, I ask myself once more what had been the secret of such perfection. One had taken it for granted at the time, for anything that is supremely good produces more acceptance than surprise. I felt we were all happy, but I didn't consider how our happiness was managed. And yet there were questions to be asked, questions that strike me as singularly obvious now that there's nobody to answer them. Mr. Offord had solved the insoluble; he had, without feminine help—save in the sense that ladies were dying to come to him and that he saved the lives of several—established a salon; but

3

I might have guessed that there was a method in his madness, a law in his success. He hadn't hit it off by a mere fluke. There was an art in it all, and how was the art so hidden? Who indeed if it came to that was the occult artist? Launching this inquiry the other day I had already got hold of the tail of my reply. I was helped by the very wonder of some of the conditions that came back to me—those that used to seem as natural as sunshine in a fine climate.

How was it for instance that we never were a crowd, never either too many or too few, always the right people WITH the right people— –there must really have been no wrong people at all—always coming and going, never sticking fast nor overstaying, yet never popping in or out with an indecorous familiarity? How was it that we all sat where we wanted and moved when we wanted and met whom we wanted and escaped whom we wanted; joining, according to the accident of inclination, the general circle or falling in with a single talker on a convenient sofa? Why were all the sofas so convenient, the accidents so happy, the talkers so ready, the listeners so willing, the subjects presented to you in a rotation as quickly foreordained as the courses at dinner? A dearth of topics would have been as unheard of as a lapse in the service. These speculations couldn't fail to lead me to the fundamental truth that Brooksmith had been somehow at the bottom of the mystery. If he hadn't established the salon at least he had carried it on. Brooksmith in short was the artist!

We felt this covertly at the time, without formulating it, and were conscious, as an ordered and prosperous community, of his even– handed justice, all untainted with flunkeyism. He had none of that vulgarity—his touch was infinitely fine. The delicacy of it was clear to me on the first occasion my eyes rested, as they were so often to rest again, on the domestic revealed, in the turbid light of the street, by the opening of the house–door. I saw on the spot that though he had plenty of school he carried it without arrogance—he had remained articulate and human. L'Ecole Anglaise Mr. Offord used laughingly to call him when, later on, it happened more than once that we had some conversation about him. But I remember accusing Mr. Offord of not doing him quite ideal justice. That he wasn't one of the giants of the school, however, was admitted by my old friend, who really understood him perfectly and was devoted to him, as I shall show; which doubtless poor Brooksmith had himself felt, to his cost, when his value in the market was originally determined. The utility of his class in general is estimated by the foot and the inch, and poor Brooksmith had only about five feet three to put into circulation. He acknowledged the inadequacy of this provision, and I'm sure was penetrated with the everlasting fitness of the relation between service and stature. If HE had been Mr. Offord he certainly would have found Brooksmith wanting, and indeed the laxity of his employer on this score was one of many things he had had to condone and to which he had at last indulgently adapted himself.

I remember the old man's saying to me: "Oh my servants, if they can live with me a fortnight they can live with me for ever. But it's the first fortnight that tries 'em." It was in the first fortnight for instance that Brooksmith had had to learn that he was exposed to being addressed as "my dear fellow" and "my poor child." Strange and deep must such a probation have been to him, and he doubtless emerged from it tempered and purified. This was written to a certain extent in his appearance; in his spare brisk little person, in his cloistered white face and extraordinarily polished hair, which told of responsibility, looked as if it were kept up to the same high standard as the plate; in his small clear anxious eyes, even in the permitted, though not exactly encouraged, tuft on his chin. "He thinks me rather mad, but I've broken him in, and now he likes the place, he likes the company," said the old man. I embraced this fully after I had become aware that Brooksmith's main characteristic was a deep and shy refinement, though I remember I was rather puzzled when, on another occasion, Mr. Offord remarked: "What he likes is the talk—mingling in the conversation." I was conscious I had never seen Brooksmith permit himself this freedom, but I guessed in a moment that what Mr. Offord alluded to was a participation more intense than any speech could have represented— that of being perpetually present on a hundred legitimate pretexts, errands, necessities, and breathing the very atmosphere of criticism, the famous criticism of life. "Quite an education, sir, isn't it, sir?" he said to me one day at the foot of the stairs when he was letting me out; and I've always remembered the words and the tone as the first sign of the quickening drama of poor Brooksmith's fate. It was indeed an education, but to what was this sensitive young man of thirty-five, of the servile class, being educated?

Practically and inevitably, for the time, to companionship, to the perpetual, the even exaggerated reference and appeal of a person brought to dependence by his time of life and his infirmities and always addicted moreover—this was the exaggeration—to the art of giving you pleasure by letting you do things for him. There were certain things Mr. Offord was capable of pretending he liked you to do even when he didn't—this, I mean, if he thought YOU liked them. If it happened that you didn't either—which was rare, yet might be—of course there were cross-purposes; but Brooksmith was there to prevent their going very far. This was precisely the way he acted as moderator; he averted misunderstandings or cleared them up. He had been capable, strange as it may appear, of acquiring for this purpose an insight into the French tongue, which was often used at Mr. Offord's; for besides being habitual to most of the foreigners, and they were many, who haunted the place or arrived with letters—letters often requiring a little worried consideration, of which Brooksmith always had cognisance—it had really become the primary language of the master of the house. I don't know if all the malentendus were in French, but almost all the explanations were, and this didn't a bit prevent Brooksmith's following them. I know Mr. Offord used to read passages to him from Montaigne and Saint–Simon, for he read perpetually when alone– –when THEY were alone, that is—and Brooksmith was always about. Perhaps you'll say no wonder Mr. Offord's butler regarded him as "rather mad." However, if I'm not sure what he thought about Montaigne I'm convinced he admired Saint–Simon. A certain feeling for letters must have rubbed off on him from the mere handling of his master's books, which he was always carrying to and fro and putting back in their places.

I often noticed that if an anecdote or a quotation, much more a lively discussion, was going forward, he would, if busy with the fire or the curtains, the lamp or the tea, find a pretext for remaining in the room till the point should be reached. If his purpose was to catch it you weren't discreet, you were in fact scarce human, to call him off, and I shall never forget a look, a hard stony stare—I caught it in its passage—which, one day when there were a good many people in the room, he fastened upon the footman who was helping him in the service and who, in an undertone, had asked him some irrelevant question. It was the only manifestation of harshness I ever observed on Brooksmith's part, and I at first wondered what was the matter. Then I became conscious that Mr. Offord was relating a very curious anecdote, never before perhaps made so public, and imparted to the narrator by an eye–witness of the fact, bearing on Lord Byron's life in Italy. Nothing would induce me to reproduce it here, but Brooksmith had been in danger of losing it. If I ever should venture to reproduce it I shall feel how much I lose in not having my fellow auditor to refer to.

The first day Mr Offord's door was closed was therefore a dark date in contemporary history. It was raining hard and my umbrella was wet, but Brooksmith received it from me exactly as if this were a preliminary for going upstairs. I observed however that instead of putting it away he held it poised and trickling over the rug, and I then became aware that he was looking at me with deep acknowledging eyes—his air of universal responsibility. I immediately understood—there was scarce need of question and answer as they passed between us. When I took in that our good friend had given up as never before, though only for the occasion, I exclaimed dolefully: "What a difference it will make—and to how many people!"

"I shall be one of them, sir!" said Brooksmith; and that was the beginning of the end.

Mr. Offord came down again, but the spell was broken, the great sign being that the conversation was for the first time not directed. It wandered and stumbled, a little frightened, like a lost child—it had let go the nurse's hand. "The worst of it is that now we shall talk about my health—c'est la fin de tout," Mr. Offord said when he reappeared; and then I recognised what a note of change that would be—for he had never tolerated anything so provincial. We "ran" to each other's health as little as to the daily weather. The talk became ours, in a word—not his; and as ours, even when HE talked, it could only be inferior. In this form it was a distress to Brooksmith, whose attention now wandered from it altogether: he had so much closer a vision of his master's intimate conditions than our superficialities represented. There were better hours, and he was more in and out of the room, but I could see he was conscious of the decline, almost of the collapse, of our great institution. He seemed to wish to take counsel with me about it, to feel responsible for its going on in some form or other. When for the second period—the first had lasted several days—he had to tell me that his employer didn't receive, I half expected to hear him say after a moment "Do you think I ought to, sir, in his place?"—as he might have asked me, with the return of autumn, if I thought he had better light the drawing–room fire.

He had a resigned philosophic sense of what his guests—our guests, as I came to regard them in our colloquies—would expect. His feeling was that he wouldn't absolutely have approved of himself as a substitute for Mr. Offord; but he was so saturated with the religion of habit that he would have made, for our friends, the necessary sacrifice to the divinity. He would take them on a little further and till they could look about them. I think I saw him also mentally confronted with the opportunity to deal—for once in his life—with some of his own dumb preferences, his limitations of sympathy, WEEDING a little in prospect and returning to a purer tradition. It was not unknown to me that he considered that toward the end of our host's career a certain laxity of selection had crept in.

At last it came to be the case that we all found the closed door more often than the open one; but even when it was closed Brooksmith managed a crack for me to squeeze through; so that practically I never turned away without having paid a visit. The difference simply came to be that the visit was to Brooksmith. It took place in the hall, at the familiar foot of the stairs, and we didn't sit down, at least Brooksmith didn't; moreover it was devoted wholly to one topic and always had the air of being already over—beginning, so to say, at the end. But it was always interesting—it always gave me something to think about. It's true that the subject of my meditation was ever the same—ever "It's all very well, but what WILL become of Brooksmith?" Even my private answer to this question left me still unsatisfied. No doubt Mr. Offord would provide for him, but WHAT would he provide?—that was the great point. He couldn't provide society; and society had become a necessity of Brooksmith's nature. I must add that he never showed a symptom of what I may call sordid solicitude— anxiety on his own account. He was rather livid and intensely grave, as befitted a man before whose eyes the "shade of that which once was great" was passing away. He had the solemnity of a person winding up, under depressing circumstances, a long–established and celebrated business; he was a kind of social executor or liquidator. But his manner seemed to testify exclusively to the uncertainty of OUR future. I couldn't in those days have afforded it—I lived in two rooms in Jermyn Street and didn't "keep a man"; but even if my income had permitted I shouldn't have ventured to say to Brooksmith (emulating Mr. Offord) "My dear fellow, I'll take you on." The whole tone of our intercourse was so much more an implication that it was I who should now want a lift. Indeed there was a tacit assurance in Brooksmith's whole attitude that he should have me on his mind.

One of the most assiduous members of our circle had been Lady Kenyon, and I remember his telling me one day that her ladyship had in spite of her own infirmities, lately much aggravated, been in person to inquire. In answer to this I remarked that she would feel it more than any one. Brooksmith had a pause before saying in a certain tone—there's no reproducing some of his tones—"I'll go and see her." I went to see her myself and learned he had waited on her; but when I said to her, in the form of a joke but with a core of earnest, that when all was over some of us ought to combine, to club together, and set Brooksmith up on his own account, she replied a trifle disappointingly: "Do you mean in a public–house?" I looked at her in a way that I think Brooksmith himself would have approved, and then I answered: "Yes, the Offord Arms." What I had meant of course was that for the love of art itself we ought to look to it that such a peculiar faculty and so much acquired experience shouldn't be wasted. I really think that if we had caused a few black—edged cards to be struck off and circulated—"Mr. Brooksmith will continue to receive on the old premises from four to seven; business carried on as usual during the alterations"—the greater number of us would have rallied.

Several times he took me upstairs—always by his own proposal—and our dear old friend, in bed (in a curious flowered and brocaded casaque which made him, especially as his head was tied up in a handkerchief to match, look, to my imagination, like the dying Voltaire) held for ten minutes a sadly shrunken little salon. I felt indeed each time as if I were attending the last coucher of some social sovereign. He was royally whimsical about his sufferings and not at all concerned—quite as if the Constitution provided for the case about his successor. He glided over OUR sufferings charmingly, and none of his jokes—it was a gallant abstention, some of them would have been so easy—were at our expense. Now and again, I confess, there was one at Brooksmith's, but so pathetically sociable as to make the excellent man look at me in a way that seemed to say: "Do exchange a glance with me, or I shan't be able to stand it." What he wasn't able to stand was not what Mr. Offord said about him, but what he wasn't able to say in return. His idea of conversation for himself was giving you the convenience of speaking to him; and when he went to "see" Lady Kenyon for instance it was to carry her the tribute of his receptive silence. Where would the speech of his betters have been if proper service had been a manifestation of sound? In that case the fundamental difference would have had to be shown by their dumbness, and many of them, poor things, were dumb enough without that provision. Brooksmith took an unfailing interest in the preservation of the fundamental difference; it was the thing he had most on his conscience.

What had become of it however when Mr. Offord passed away like any inferior person—was relegated to eternal stillness after the manner of a butler above–stairs? His aspect on the event—for the several successive days—may be imagined, and the multiplication by funereal observance of the things he didn't say. When everything was over—it was late the same day—I knocked at the door of the house of mourning as I so often had done before. I could never call on Mr. Offord again, but I had come literally to call on Brooksmith. I wanted to ask him if there was anything I could do for him, tainted with vagueness as this inquiry could only be. My presumptuous dream of taking him into my own service had died away: my service wasn't worth his being taken into. My offer could only be to help him to find another place, and yet there was an indelicacy, as it were, in taking for granted that his thoughts would immediately be fixed on another. I had a hope that he would be able to give his life a different form—though certainly not the form, the frequent result of such bereavements, of his setting up a little shop. That would have been dreadful; for I should have wished to forward any enterprise he might embark in, yet how could I have brought myself to go and pay him shillings and take back coppers, over a counter? My visit then was simply an intended compliment. He took it as such, gratefully and with all the tact in the world. He knew I really couldn't help him and that I knew he knew I couldn't; but we discussed the situation—with a good deal of elegant generality—at the foot of the stairs, in the hall already dismantled, where I had so often discussed other situations with him. The executors were in possession, as was still more apparent when he made me pass for a few minutes into the dining– room, where various objects were muffled up for removal.

Two definite facts, however, he had to communicate; one being that he was to leave the house for ever that night (servants, for some mysterious reason, seem always to depart by night), and the other— he mentioned it only at the last and with hesitation—that he was already aware his late master had left him a legacy of eighty pounds. "I'm very glad," I said, and Brooksmith was of the same mind: "It was so like him to think of me." This was all that passed between us on the subject, and I know nothing of his judgement of Mr. Offord's memento. Eighty pounds are always eighty pounds, and no one has ever left ME an equal sum; but, all the same, for Brooksmith, I was disappointed. I don't know what I had expected, but it was almost a shock. Eighty pounds might stock a small shop—a VERY small shop; but, I repeat, I couldn't bear to think of that. I asked my friend if he had been able to save a little, and he replied: "No, sir; I've had to do things." I didn't inquire what things they might have been; they were his own affair, and I took his word for them as assentingly as if he had had the greatness of an ancient house to keep up; especially as there was something in his manner that seemed to convey a prospect of further sacrifice.

"I shall have to turn round a bit, sir—I shall have to look about me," he said; and then he added indulgently, magnanimously: "If you should happen to hear of anything for me—"

I couldn't let him finish; this was, in its essence, too much in the really grand manner. It would be a help to my getting him off my mind to be able to pretend I COULD find the right place, and that help he wished to give me, for it was doubtless painful to him to see me in so false a position. I interposed with a few words to the effect of how well aware I was that wherever he should go, whatever he should do, he would miss our old friend terribly—miss him even more than I should, having been with him so much more. This led him to make the speech that has remained with me as the very text of the whole episode.

"Oh sir, it's sad for YOU, very sad indeed, and for a great many gentlemen and ladies; that it is, sir. But for me, sir, it is, if I may say so, still graver even than that: it's just the loss of something that was everything. For me, sir," he went on with rising tears, "he was just ALL, if you know what I mean, sir. You have others, sir, I daresay—not that I would have you understand me to speak of them as in any way tantamount. But you have the pleasures of society, sir; if it's only in talking about him, sir, as I daresay you do freely—for all his blest memory has to fear from it—with gentlemen and ladies who have had the same honour. That's not for me, sir, and I've to keep my associations to myself. Mr. Offord was MY society, and now, you see, I just haven't any. You go back to conversation, sir, after all, and I go back to my place," Brooksmith stammered, without exaggerated irony or dramatic bitterness, but with a flat unstudied veracity and his hand on the knob of the street–door. He turned it to let me out and then he added: "I just go downstairs, sir, again, and I stay there."

"My poor child," I replied in my emotion, quite as Mr. Offord used to speak, "my dear fellow, leave it to me: WE'LL look after you, we'll all do something for you."

"Ah if you could give me some one LIKE him! But there ain't two such in the world," Brooksmith said as we parted.

He had given me his address—the place where he would be to be heard of. For a long time I had no occasion to make use of the information: he proved on trial so very difficult a case. The people who knew him and had known Mr. Offord didn't want to take him, and yet I couldn't bear to try to thrust him among strangers— strangers to his past when not to his present. I spoke to many of our old friends about him and found them all governed by the odd mixture of feelings of which I myself was conscious—as well as disposed, further, to entertain a suspicion that he was "spoiled," with which, I then would have nothing to do. In plain terms a certain embarrassment, a sensible awkwardness when they thought of it, attached to the idea of using him as a menial: they had met him so often in society. Many of them would have asked him, and did ask him, or rather did ask me to ask him, to come and see them, but a mere visiting–list was not what I wanted for him. He was too short for people who were very particular; nevertheless I heard of an opening in a diplomatic household which led me to write him a note, though I was looking much less for something grand than for something human. Five days later I heard from him. The secretary's wife had decided, after keeping him waiting till then, that she couldn't take a servant out of a house in which there hadn't been a lady. The note had a P.S.: "It's a good job there wasn't, sir, such a lady as some."

A week later he came to see me and told me he was "suited," committed to some highly respectable people—they were something quite immense in the City—who lived on the Bayswater side of the Park. "I daresay it will be rather poor, sir," he admitted; "but I've seen the fireworks, haven't I, sir?—it can't be fireworks EVERY night. After Mansfield Street there ain't much choice." There was a certain amount, however, it seemed; for the following year, calling one day on a country cousin, a lady of a certain age who was spending a fortnight in town with some friends of her own, a family unknown to me and resident in Chester Square, the door of the house was opened, to my surprise and gratification, by Brooksmith in person. When I came out I had some conversation with him from which I gathered that he had found the large City people too dull for endurance, and I guessed, though he didn't say it, that he had found them vulgar as well. I don't know what judgement he would have passed on his actual patrons if my relative hadn't been their friend; but in view of that connexion he abstained from comment.

None was necessary, however, for before the lady in question brought her visit to a close they honoured me with an invitation to dinner, which I accepted. There was a largeish party on the occasion, but I confess I thought of Brooksmith rather more than of the seated company. They required no depth of attention—they were all referable to usual irredeemable inevitable types. It was the world of cheerful commonplace and conscious gentility and prosperous density, a full−fed material insular world, a world of hideous florid plate and ponderous order and thin conversation. There wasn't a word said about Byron, or even about a minor bard then much in view. Nothing would have induced me to look at Brooksmith in the course of the repast, and I felt sure that not even my overturning the wine would have induced him to meet my eye. We were in intellectual sympathy—we felt, as regards each other, a degree of social responsibility. In short we had been in Arcadia together, and we had both come to THIS! No wonder we were ashamed to be confronted. When he had helped on my overcoat, as I was going away, we parted, for the first time since the earliest days of Mansfield Street, in silence. I thought he looked lean and wasted, and I guessed that his new place wasn't more "human" than his previous one. There was plenty of beef and beer, but there was no reciprocity. The question for him to have asked before accepting the position wouldn't have been "How many footmen are kept?" but "How much imagination?"

The next time I went to the house—I confess it wasn't very soon—I encountered his successor, a personage who evidently enjoyed the good fortune of never having quitted his natural level. Could any be higher? he seemed to ask—over the heads of three footmen and even of some visitors. He made me feel as if Brooksmith were dead; but I didn't dare to inquire—I couldn't have borne his "I haven't the least idea, sir." I despatched a note to the address that worthy had given me after Mr. Offord's death, but I received no answer. Six months later however I was favoured with a visit from an elderly dreary dingy person who introduced herself to me as Mr. Brooksmith's aunt and from whom I learned that he was out of place and out of health and had allowed her to come and say to me that if I could spare half an hour to look in at him he would take it as a rare honour.

I went the next day—his messenger had given me a new address—and found my friend lodged in a short sordid street in Marylebone, one of those corners of London that wear the last expression of sickly meanness. The room into which I was shown was above the small establishment of a dyer and cleaner who had inflated kid gloves and discoloured shawls in his shop-front. There was a great deal of grimy infant life up and down the place, and there was a hot moist smell within, as of the "boiling" of dirty linen. Brooksmith sat with a blanket over his legs at a clean little window where, from behind stiff bluish-white curtains, he could look across at a huckster's and a tinsmith's and a small greasy public-house. He had passed through an illness and was convalescent, and his mother, as well as his aunt, was in attendance on him. I liked the nearer relative, who was bland and intensely humble, but I had my doubts of the remoter, whom I connected perhaps unjustly with the opposite public-house—she seemed somehow greasy with the same grease—and whose furtive eye followed every movement of my hand as to see if it weren't going into my pocket. It didn't take this direction—I couldn't, unsolicited, put myself at that sort of ease with Brooksmith. Several times the door of the room opened and mysterious old women peeped in and shuffled back again. I don't know who they were; poor Brooksmith seemed encompassed with vague prying beery females.

He was vague himself, and evidently weak, and much embarrassed, and not an allusion was made between us to Mansfield Street. The vision of the salon of which he had been an ornament hovered before me however, by contrast, sufficiently. He assured me he was really getting better, and his mother remarked that he would come round if he could only get his spirits up. The aunt echoed this opinion, and I became more sure that in her own case she knew where to go for such a purpose. I'm afraid I was rather weak with my old friend, for I neglected the opportunity, so exceptionally good, to rebuke the levity which had led him to throw up honourable positions—fine stiff steady berths in Bayswater and Belgravia, with morning prayers, as I knew, attached to one of them. Very likely his reasons had been profane and sentimental; he didn't want morning prayers, he wanted to be somebody's dear fellow; but I couldn't be the person to rebuke him. He shuffled these episodes out of sight—I saw he had no wish to discuss them. I noted further, strangely enough, that it would probably be a questionable pleasure for him to see me again: he doubted now even of my power to condone his aberrations. He didn't wish to have to explain; and his behaviour was likely in future to need explanation. When I bade him farewell he looked at me a moment with eyes that said everything: "How can I talk about those exquisite years in this place, before these people, with the old women poking their heads in? It was very good of you to come to see me; it wasn't my idea— SHE brought you. We've said everything; it's over; you'll lose all patience with me, and I'd rather you shouldn't see the rest." I sent him some money in a letter the next day, but I saw the rest only in the light of a barren sequel.

A whole year after my visit to him I became aware once, in dining out, that Brooksmith was one of the several servants who hovered behind our chairs. He hadn't opened the door of the house to me, nor had I recognised him in the array of retainers in the hall. This time I tried to catch his eye, but he never gave me a chance, and when he handed me a dish I could only be careful to thank him audibly. Indeed I partook of two entrees of which I had my doubts, subsequently converted into certainties, in order not to snub him. He looked well enough in health, but much older, and wore in an exceptionally marked degree the glazed and expressionless mask of the British domestic de race. I saw with dismay that if I hadn't known him I should have taken him, on the showing of his countenance, for an extravagant illustration of irresponsive servile gloom. I said to myself that he had become a reactionary, gone over to the Philistines, thrown himself into religion, the religion of his "place," like a foreign lady sur le retour. I divined moreover that he was only engaged for the evening—he had become a mere waiter, had joined the band of the white–waistcoated who "go out." There was something pathetic in this fact—it was a terrible vulgarisation of Brooksmith. It was the mercenary prose of butlerhood; he had given up the struggle for the poetry. If reciprocity was what he had missed where was the reciprocity now? Only in the bottoms of the wine–glasses and the five shillings—or whatever they get—clapped into his hand by the permanent man.

However, I supposed he had taken up a precarious branch of his profession because it after all sent him less downstairs. His relations with London society were more superficial, but they were of course more various. As I went away on this occasion I looked out for him eagerly among the four or five attendants whose perpendicular persons, fluting the walls of London passages, are supposed to lubricate the process of departure; but he was not on duty. I asked one of the others if he were not in the house, and received the prompt answer: "Just left, sir. Anything I can do for you, sir?" I wanted to say "Please give him my kind regards"; but I abstained—I didn't want to compromise him; and I never came across him again.

Often and often, in dining out, I looked for him, sometimes accepting invitations on purpose to multiply the chances of my meeting him. But always in vain; so that as I met many other members of the casual class over and over again I at last adopted the theory that he always procured a list of expected guests beforehand and kept away from the banquets which he thus learned I was to grace. At last I gave up hope, and one day at the end of three years I received another visit from his aunt. She was drearier and dingier, almost squalid, and she was in great tribulation and want. Her sister, Mrs. Brooksmith, had been dead a year, and three months later her nephew had disappeared. He had always looked after her a bit since her troubles; I never knew what her troubles had been—and now she hadn't so much as a petticoat to pawn. She had also a niece, to whom she had been everything before her troubles, but the niece had treated her most shameful. These were details; the great and romantic fact was Brooksmith's final evasion of his fate. He had gone out to wait one evening as usual, in a white waistcoat she had done up for him with her own hands— being due at a large party up Kensington way. But he had never come home again and had never arrived at the large party, nor at any party that any one could make out. No trace of him had come to light—no gleam of the white waistcoat had pierced the obscurity of his doom. This news was a sharp shock to me, for I had my ideas about his real destination. His aged relative had promptly, as she said, guessed the worst. Somehow, and somewhere he had got out of the way altogether, and now I trust that, with characteristic deliberation, he is changing the plates of the immortal gods. As my depressing visitant also said, he never HAD got his spirits up. I was fortunately able to dismiss her with her own somewhat improved. But the dim ghost of poor Brooksmith is one of those that I see. He had indeed been spoiled.

THE REAL THING

CHAPTER I

When the porter's wife, who used to answer the house–bell, announced "A gentleman and a lady, sir," I had, as I often had in those days—the wish being father to the thought—an immediate vision of sitters. Sitters my visitors in this case proved to be; but not in the sense I should have preferred. There was nothing at first however to indicate that they mightn't have come for a portrait. The gentleman, a man of fifty, very high and very straight, with a moustache slightly grizzled and a dark grey walking–coat admirably fitted, both of which I noted professionally—I don't mean as a barber or yet as a tailor—would have struck me as a celebrity if celebrities often were striking. It was a truth of which I had for some time been conscious that a figure with a good deal of frontage was, as one might say, almost never a public institution. A glance at the lady helped to remind me of this paradoxical law: she also looked too distinguished to be a "personality." Moreover one would scarcely come across two variations together.

Neither of the pair immediately spoke—they only prolonged the preliminary gaze suggesting that each wished to give the other a chance. They were visibly shy; they stood there letting me take them in—which, as I afterwards perceived, was the most practical thing they could have done. In this way their embarrassment served their cause. I had seen people painfully reluctant to mention that they desired anything so gross as to be represented on canvas; but the scruples of my new friends appeared almost insurmountable. Yet the gentleman might have said "I should like a portrait of my wife," and the lady might have said "I should like a portrait of my husband." Perhaps they weren't husband and wife—this naturally would make the matter more delicate. Perhaps they wished to be done together—in which case they ought to have brought a third person to break the news.

"We come from Mr. Rivet," the lady finally said with a dim smile that had the effect of a moist sponge passed over a "sunk" piece of painting, as well as of a vague allusion to vanished beauty. She was as tall and straight, in her degree, as her companion, and with ten years less to carry. She looked as sad as a woman could look whose face was not charged with expression; that is her tinted oval mask showed waste as an exposed surface shows friction. The hand of time had played over her freely, but to an effect of elimination. She was slim and stiff, and so well–dressed, in dark blue cloth, with lappets and pockets and buttons, that it was clear she employed the same tailor as her husband. The couple had an indefinable air of prosperous thrift—they evidently got a good deal of luxury for their money. If I was to be one of their luxuries it would behove me to consider my terms.

"Ah Claude Rivet recommended me?" I echoed and I added that it was very kind of him, though I could reflect that, as he only painted landscape, this wasn't a sacrifice.

The lady looked very hard at the gentleman, and the gentleman looked round the room. Then staring at the floor a moment and stroking his moustache, he rested his pleasant eyes on me with the remark: "He said you were the right one."

"I try to be, when people want to sit."

"Yes, we should like to," said the lady anxiously.

"Do you mean together?"

My visitors exchanged a glance. "If you could do anything with ME I suppose it would be double," the gentleman stammered.

"Oh yes, there's naturally a higher charge for two figures than for one."

"We should like to make it pay," the husband confessed.

"That's very good of you," I returned, appreciating so unwonted a sympathy—for I supposed he meant pay the artist.

A sense of strangeness seemed to dawn on the lady. "We mean for the illustrations—Mr. Rivet said you might put one in."

"Put in—an illustration?" I was equally confused.

"Sketch her off, you know," said the gentleman, colouring.

Some Short Stories

It was only then that I understood the service Claude Rivet had rendered me; he had told them how I worked in black–and–white, for magazines, for story–books, for sketches of contemporary life, and consequently had copious employment for models. These things were true, but it was not less true—I may confess it now; whether because the aspiration was to lead to everything or to nothing I leave the reader to guess—that I couldn't get the honours, to say nothing of the emoluments, of a great painter of portraits out of my head. My "illustrations" were my pot–boilers; I looked to a different branch of art—far and away the most interesting it had always seemed to me—to perpetuate my fame. There was no shame in looking to it also to make my fortune but that fortune was by so much further from being made from the moment my visitors wished to be "done" for nothing. I was disappointed; for in the pictorial sense I had immediately SEEN them. I had seized their type—I had already settled what I would do with it. Something that wouldn't absolutely have pleased them, I afterwards reflected.

"Ah you're—you're—a –?" I began as soon as I had mastered my surprise. I couldn't bring out the dingy word "models": it seemed so little to fit the case.

"We haven't had much practice," said the lady.

"We've got to do something, and we've thought that an artist in your line might perhaps make something of us," her husband threw off. He further mentioned that they didn't know many artists and that they had gone first, on the off–chance—he painted views of course, but sometimes put in figures; perhaps I remembered—to Mr. Rivet, whom they had met a few years before at a place in Norfolk where he was sketching.

"We used to sketch a little ourselves," the lady hinted.

"It's very awkward, but we absolutely must do something," her husband went on.

"Of course we're not so VERY young," she admitted with a wan smile.

With the remark that I might as well know something more about them the husband had handed me a card extracted from a neat new pocket- book—their appurtenances were all of the freshest—and inscribed with the words "Major Monarch." Impressive as these words were they didn't carry my knowledge much further; but my visitor presently added: "I've left the army and we've had the misfortune to lose our money. In fact our means are dreadfully small."

"It's awfully trying—a regular strain,", said Mrs. Monarch.

They evidently wished to be discreet—to take care not to swagger because they were gentlefolk. I felt them willing to recognise this as something of a drawback, at the same time that I guessed at an underlying sense—their consolation in adversity—that they HAD their points. They certainly had; but these advantages struck me as preponderantly social; such for instance as would help to make a drawing–room look well. However, a drawing–room was always, or ought to be, a picture.

In consequence of his wife's allusion to their age Major Monarch observed: "Naturally it's more for the figure that we thought of going in. We can still hold ourselves up." On the instant I saw that the figure was indeed their strong point. His "naturally" didn't sound vain, but it lighted up the question. "SHE has the best one," he continued, nodding at his wife with a pleasant after– dinner absence of circumlocution. I could only reply, as if we were in fact sitting over our wine, that this didn't prevent his own from being very good; which led him in turn to make answer: "We thought that if you ever have to do people like us we might be something like it. SHE particularly—for a lady in a book, you know."

I was so amused by them that, to get more of it, I did my best to take their point of view; and though it was an embarrassment to find myself appraising physically, as if they were animals on hire or useful blacks, a pair whom I should have expected to meet only in one of the relations in which criticism is tacit, I looked at Mrs. Monarch judicially enough to be able to exclaim after a moment with conviction: "Oh yes, a lady in a book!" She was singularly like a bad illustration.

"We'll stand up, if you like," said the Major; and he raised himself before me with a really grand air.

I could take his measure at a glance—he was six feet two and a perfect gentleman. It would have paid any club in process of formation and in want of a stamp to engage him at a salary to stand in the principal window. What struck me at once was that in coming to me they had rather missed their vocation; they could surely have been turned to better account for advertising purposes. I couldn't of course see the thing in detail, but I could see them make somebody's fortune—I don't mean their own. There was something in them for a waistcoat–maker, an hotel–keeper or a soap–vendor. I could imagine "We always use it" pinned on their bosoms with the greatest effect; I had a vision of the brilliancy with which they would launch a table d'hote.

Mrs. Monarch sat still, not from pride but from shyness, and presently her husband said to her: "Get up, my dear, and show how smart you are." She obeyed, but she had no need to get up to show it. She walked to the end of the studio and then came back blushing, her fluttered eyes on the partner of her appeal. I was reminded of an incident I had accidentally had a glimpse of in Paris—being with a friend there, a dramatist about to produce a play, when an actress came to him to ask to be entrusted with a part. She went through her paces before him, walked up and down as Mrs. Monarch was doing. Mrs. Monarch did it quite as well, but I abstained from applauding. It was very odd to see such people apply for such poor pay. She looked as if she had ten thousand a year. Her husband had used the word that described her: she was in the London current jargon essentially and typically "smart." Her figure was, in the same order of ideas, conspicuously and irreproachably "good." For a woman of her age her waist was surprisingly small; her elbow moreover had the orthodox crook. She held her head at the conventional angle, but why did she come to ME? She ought to have tried on jackets at a big shop. I feared my visitors were not only destitute but "artistic"—which would be a great complication. When she sat down again I thanked her, observing that what a draughtsman most valued in his model was the faculty of keeping quiet.

"Oh SHE can keep quiet," said Major Monarch. Then he added jocosely: "I've always kept her quiet."

"I'm not a nasty fidget, am I?" It was going to wring tears from me, I felt, the way she hid her head, ostrich–like, in the other broad bosom.

The owner of this expanse addressed his answer to me. "Perhaps it isn't out of place to mention—because we ought to be quite business–like, oughtn't we?—that when I married her she was known as the Beautiful Statue."

"Oh dear!" said Mrs. Monarch ruefully.

"Of course I should want a certain amount of expression," I rejoined.

"Of COURSE!"—and I had never heard such unanimity.

"And then I suppose you know that you'll get awfully tired."

"Oh we NEVER get tired!" they eagerly cried.

"Have you had any kind of practice?"

They hesitated—they looked at each other. We've been photographed—IMMENSELY," said Mrs. Monarch.

"She means the fellows have asked us themselves," added the Major.

"I see—because you're so good–looking."

"I don't know what they thought, but they were always after us."

"We always got our photographs for nothing,"

smiled Mrs. Monarch.

"We might have brought some, my dear," her husband remarked.

"I'm not sure we have any left. We've given quantities away," she explained to me.

"With our autographs and that sort of thing," said the Major.

"Are they to be got in the shops?" I inquired as a harmless pleasantry.

"Oh yes, HERS—they used to be."

"Not now," said Mrs. Monarch with her eyes on the floor.

CHAPTER II

I could fancy the "sort of thing" they put on the presentation copies of their photographs, and I was sure they wrote a beautiful hand. It was odd how quickly I was sure of everything that concerned them. If they were now so poor as to have to cam shillings and pence they could never have had much of a margin. Their good looks had been their capital, and they had good– humouredly made the most of the career that this resource marked out for them. It was in their faces, the blankness, the deep intellectual repose of the twenty years of country–house visiting that had given them pleasant intonations. I could see the sunny drawing–rooms, sprinkled with periodicals she didn't read, in which Mrs. Monarch had continuously sat; I could see the wet shrubberies in which she had walked, equipped to admiration for either exercise. I could see the rich covers the Major had helped to shoot and the wonderful garments in which, late at night, he repaired to the smoking–room to talk about them. I could imagine their leggings and waterproofs, their knowing tweeds and rugs, their rolls of sticks and cases of tackle and neat umbrellas; and I could evoke the exact appearance of their servants and the compact variety of their luggage on the platforms of country stations.

They gave small tips, but they were liked; they didn't do anything themselves, but they were welcome. They looked so well everywhere; they gratified the general relish for stature, complexion and "form." They knew it without fatuity or vulgarity, and they respected themselves in consequence. They weren't superficial: they were thorough and kept themselves up—it had been their line. People with such a taste for activity had to have some line. I could feel how even in a dull house they could have been counted on for the joy of life. At present something had happened—it didn't matter what, their little income had grown less, it had grown least—and they had to do something for pocket–money. Their friends could like them, I made out, without liking to support them. There was something about them that represented credit— their clothes, their manners, their type; but if credit is a large empty pocket in which an occasional chink reverberates, the chink at least must be audible. What they wanted of me was help to make it so. Fortunately they had no children—I soon divined that. They would also perhaps wish our relations to be kept secret: this was why it was "for the figure"—the reproduction of the face would betray them.

I liked them—I felt, quite as their friends must have done—they were so simple; and I had no objection to them if they would suit. But somehow with all their perfections I didn't easily believe in them. After all they were amateurs, and the ruling passion of my life was—the detestation of the amateur. Combined with this was another perversity—an innate preference for the represented subject over the real one: the defect of the real one was so apt to be a lack of representation. I liked things that appeared; then one was sure. Whether they WERE or not was a subordinate and almost always a profitless question. There were other considerations, the first of which was that I already had two or three recruits in use, notably a young person with big feet, in alpaca, from Kilburn, who for a couple of years had come to me regularly for my illustrations and with whom I was still—perhaps ignobly—satisfied. I frankly explained to my visitors how the case stood, but they had taken more precautions than I supposed. They had reasoned out their opportunity, for Claude Rivet had told them of the projected edition de luxe of one of the writers of our day—the rarest of the novelists—who, long neglected by the multitudinous vulgar, and dearly prized by the attentive (need I mention Philip Vincent?) had had the happy fortune of seeing, late in life, the dawn and then the full light of a higher criticism; an estimate in which on the part of the public there was something really of expiation. The edition preparing, planned by a publisher of taste, was practically an act of high reparation; the woodcuts with which it was to be enriched were the homage of English art to one of the most independent representatives of English letters. Major and Mrs. Monarch confessed to me they had hoped I might be able to work THEM into my branch of the enterprise. They knew I was to do the first of the books, Rutland Ramsay, but I had to make clear to them that my participation in the rest of the affair—this first book was to be a test—must depend on the satisfaction I should give. If this should be limited my employers would drop me with scarce common forms. It was therefore a crisis for me, and naturally I was making special preparations, looking about for new people, should they be necessary, and securing the best types. I admitted however that I should like to settle down to two or three good models who would do for everything.

"Should we have often to—a—put on special clothes?" Mrs. Monarch timidly demanded.

"Dear yes—that's half the business."

"And should we be expected to supply our own costumes?

"Oh no; I've got a lot of things. A painter's models put on—or put off—anything he likes."

Some Short Stories

"And you mean—a—the same?"

"The same?"

Mrs. Monarch looked at her husband again.

"Oh she was just wondering," he explained, "if the costumes are in GENERAL use." I had to confess that they were, and I mentioned further that some of them—I had a lot of, genuine greasy last– century things—had served their time, a hundred years ago, on living world–stained men and women; on figures not perhaps so far removed, in that vanished world, from THEIR type, the Monarchs', quoi! of a breeched and bewigged age. "We'll put, on anything that FITS," said the Major.

"Oh I arrange that—they fit in the pictures."

"I'm afraid I should do better for the modern books. I'd come as you like," said Mrs. Monarch.

"She has got a lot of clothes at home: they might do for contemporary life," her husband continued.

"Oh I can fancy scenes in which you'd be quite natural." And indeed I could see the slipshod re–arrangements of stale properties—the stories I tried to produce pictures for without the exasperation of reading them—whose sandy tracts the good lady might help to people. But I had to return to the fact that—for this sort of work—the daily mechanical grind—I was already equipped: the people I was working with wore fully adequate.

"We only thought we might be more like SOME characters," said Mrs. Monarch mildly, getting up.

Her husband also rose; he stood looking at me with a dim wistfulness that was touching in so fine a man. "Wouldn't it be rather a pull sometimes to have—a—to haven?" He hung fire; he wanted me to help him by phrasing what he meant. But I couldn't—I didn't know. So he brought it out awkwardly: "The REAL thing; a gentleman, you know, or a lady." I was quite ready to give a general assent—I admitted that there was a great deal in that. This encouraged Major Monarch to say, following up his appeal with an unacted gulp: "It's awfully hard—we've tried everything." The gulp was communicative; it proved too much for his wife. Before I knew it Mrs. Monarch had dropped again upon a divan and burst into tears. Her husband sat down beside her, holding one of her hands; whereupon she quickly dried her eyes with the other, while I felt embarrassed as she looked up at me. "There isn't a confounded job I haven't applied for—waited for—prayed for. You can fancy we'd be pretty bad first. Secretaryships and that sort of thing? You might as well ask for a peerage. I'd be ANYTHING—I'm strong; a messenger or a coalheaver. I'd put on a gold–laced cap and open carriage–doors in front of the haberdasher's; I'd hang about a station to carry portmanteaux; I'd be a postman. But they won't LOOK at you; there are thousands as good as yourself already on the ground. GENTLEMEN, poor beggars, who've drunk their wine, who've kept their hunters!"

I was as reassuring as I knew how to be, and my visitors were presently on their feet again while, for the experiment, we agreed on an hour. We were discussing it when the door opened and Miss Churm came in with a wet umbrella. Miss Churm had to take the omnibus to Maida Vale and then walk half a mile. She looked a trifle blowsy and slightly splashed. I scarcely ever saw her come in without thinking afresh how odd it was that, being so little in herself, she should yet be so much in others. She was a meagre little Miss Churm, but was such an ample heroine of romance. She was only a freckled cockney, but she could represent everything, from a fine lady to a shepherdess, she had the faculty as she might have had a fine voice or long hair. She couldn't spell and she loved beer, but she had two or three "points," and practice, and a knack, and mother–wit, and a whimsical sensibility, and a love of the theatre, and seven sisters,—and not an ounce of respect, especially for the H. The first thing my visitors saw was that her umbrella was wet, and in their spotless perfection they visibly winced at it. The rain had come on since their arrival.

"I'm all in a soak; there WAS a mess of people in the 'bus. I wish you lived near a stytion," said Miss Churm. I requested her to get ready as quickly as possible, and she passed into the room in which she always changed her dress. But before going out she asked me what she was to get into this time.

"It's the Russian princess, don't you know?" I answered; "the one with the 'golden eyes,' in black velvet, for the long thing in the Cheapside."

"Golden eyes? I SAY!" cried Miss Churm, while my companions watched her with intensity as she withdrew. She always arranged herself, when she was late, before I could turn round; and I kept my visitors a little on purpose, so that they might get an idea, from seeing her, what would be expected of themselves. I mentioned that she was quite my notion of ail excellent model—she was really very clever.

"Do you think she looks like a Russian princess?" Major Monarch asked with lurking alarm.

"When I make her, yes."

"Oh if you have to MAKE her—!" he reasoned, not without point.

"That's the most you can ask. There are so many who are not makeable."

"Well now, HERE'S a lady"—and with a persuasive smile he passed his arm into his wife's—"who's already made!"

"Oh I'm not a Russian princess," Mrs. Monarch protested a little coldly. I could see she had known some and didn't like them. There at once was a complication of a kind I never had to fear with Miss Churm.

This young lady came back in black velvet—the gown was rather rusty and very low on her lean shoulders—and with a Japanese fan in her red hands. I reminded her that in the scene I was doing she had to look over some one's head. "I forget whose it is but it doesn't matter. Just look over a head."

"I'd rather look over a stove," said Miss Churm and she took her station near the fire. She fell into Position, settled herself into a tall attitude, gave a certain backward inclination to her head and a certain forward droop to her fan, and looked, at least to my prejudiced sense, distinguished and charming, foreign and dangerous. We left her looking so while I went downstairs with Major and Mrs. Monarch.

"I believe I could come about as near it as that," said Mrs. Monarch.

"Oh you think she's shabby, but you must allow for the alchemy of art."

However, they went off with an evident increase of comfort founded on their demonstrable advantage in being the real thing. I could fancy them shuddering over Miss Churm. She was very droll about them when I went back, for I told her what they wanted.

"Well, if SHE can sit I'll tyke to bookkeeping," said my model.

"She's very ladylike," I replied as an innocent form of aggravation.

"So much the worse for YOU. That means she can't turn round."

"She'll do for the fashionable novels."

"Oh yes, she'll DO for them!" my model humorously declared. "Ain't they bad enough without her?" I had often sociably denounced them to Miss Churm.

CHAPTER III

It was for the elucidation of a mystery in one of these works that I first tried Mrs. Monarch. Her husband came with her, to be useful if necessary—it was sufficiently clear that as a general thing he would prefer to come with her. At first I wondered if this were for "propriety's" sake—if he were going to be jealous and meddling. The idea was too tiresome, and if it had been confirmed it would speedily have brought our acquaintance to a close. But I soon saw there was nothing in it and that if he accompanied Mrs. Monarch it was—in addition to the chance of being wanted—simply because he had nothing else to do. When they were separate his occupation was gone, and they never HAD been separate. I judged rightly that in their awkward situation their close union was their main comfort and that this union had no weak spot. It was a real marriage, an encouragement to the hesitating, a nut for pessimists to crack. Their address was humble—I remember afterwards thinking it had been the only thing about them that was really professional—and I could fancy the lamentable lodgings in which the Major would have been left alone. He could sit there more or less grimly with his wife—he couldn't sit there anyhow without her.

He had too much tact to try and make himself agreeable when he couldn't be useful; so when I was too absorbed in my work to talk he simply sat and waited. But I liked to hear him talk—it made my work, when not interrupting it, less mechanical, less special. To listen to him was to combine the excitement of going out with the economy of staying at home. There was only one hindrance—that I seemed not to know any of the people this brilliant couple had known. I think he wondered extremely, during the term of our intercourse, whom the deuce I DID know. He hadn't a stray sixpence of an idea to fumble for, so we didn't spin it very fine; we confined ourselves to questions of leather and even of liquor– saddlers and breeches–makers and how to get excellent claret cheap– –and matters like "good trains" and the habits of small game. His lore on these last subjects was astonishing—he managed to interweave the station–master with the ornithologist. When he couldn't talk about greater things he could talk cheerfully about smaller, and since I couldn't accompany him into reminiscences of the fashionable world he could lower the conversation without a visible effort to my level.

So earnest a desire to please was touching in a man who could so easily have knocked one down. He looked after the fire and had an opinion on the draught of the stove without my asking him, and I could see that he thought many of my arrangements not half knowing. I remember telling him that if I were only rich I'd offer him a salary to come and teach me how to live. Sometimes he gave a random sigh of which the essence might have been: "Give me even such a bare old–barrack as this, and I'd do something with it!" When I wanted to use him he came alone; which was an illustration of the superior courage of women. His wife could bear her solitary second floor, and she was in general more discreet; showing by various small reserves that she was alive to the propriety of keeping our relations markedly professional—not letting them slide into sociability. She wished it to remain clear that she and the Major were employed, not cultivated, and if she approved of me as a superior, who could be kept in his place, she never thought me quite good enough for an equal.

She sat with great intensity, giving the whole of her mind to it, and was capable of remaining for an hour almost as motionless as before a photographer's lens. I could see she had been photographed often, but somehow the very habit that made her good for that purpose unfitted her for mine. At first I was extremely pleased with her ladylike air, and it was a satisfaction, on coming to follow her lines, to see how good they were and how far they could lead the pencil. But after a little skirmishing I began to find her too insurmountably stiff; do what I would with it my drawing looked like a photograph or a copy of a photograph. Her figure had no variety of expression—she herself had no sense of variety. You may say that this was my business and was only a question of placing her.

28

Yet I placed her in every conceivable position and she managed to obliterate their differences. She was always a lady certainly, and into the bargain was always the same lady. She was the real thing, but always the same thing. There were moments when I rather writhed under the serenity of her confidence that she WAS the real thing. All her dealings with me and all her husband's were an implication that this was lucky for ME. Meanwhile I found myself trying to invent types that approached her own, instead of making her own transform itself—in the clever way that was not impossible for instance to poor Miss Churm. Arrange as I would and take the precautions I would, she always came out, in my pictures, too tall—landing me in the dilemma of having represented a fascinating woman as seven feet high, which (out of respect perhaps to my own very much scantier inches) was far from my idea of such a personage.

The case was worse with the Major—nothing I could do would keep HIM down, so that he became useful only for the representation of brawny giants. I adored variety and range, I cherished human accidents, the illustrative note; I wanted to characterise closely, and the thing in the world I most hated was the danger of being ridden by a type. I had quarrelled with some of my friends about it; I had parted company with them for maintaining that one HAD to be, and that if the type was beautiful—witness Raphael and Leonardo—the servitude was only a gain. I was neither Leonardo nor Raphael—I might only be a presumptuous young modern searcher; but I held that everything was to be sacrificed sooner than character. When they claimed that the obsessional form could easily BE character I retorted, perhaps superficially, "Whose?" It couldn't be everybody's—it might end in being nobody's.

After I had drawn Mrs. Monarch a dozen times I felt surer even than before that the value of such a model as Miss Churm resided precisely in the fact that she had no positive stamp, combined of course with the other fact that what she did have was a curious and inexplicable talent for imitation. Her usual appearance was like a curtain which—she could draw up at request for a capital performance. This performance was simply suggestive; but it was a word to the wise—it was vivid and pretty. Sometimes even I thought it, though she was plain herself, too insipidly pretty; I made it a reproach to her that the figures drawn from her were monotonously (betement, as we used to say) graceful. Nothing made her more angry: it was so much her pride to feel she could sit for characters that had nothing in common with each other. She would accuse me at such moments of taking away her "reputytion."

It suffered a certain shrinkage, this queer quantity, from the repeated visits of my new friends. Miss Churm was greatly in demand, never in want of employment, so I had no scruple in putting her off occasionally, to try them more at my ease. It was certainly amusing at first to do the real thing—it was amusing to do Major Monarch's trousers. They WERE the real thing, even if he did come out colossal. It was amusing to do his wife's back hair— it was so mathematically neat—and the particular "smart" tension of her tight stays. She lent herself especially to positions in which the face was somewhat averted or blurred, she abounded in ladylike back views and profils perdus. When she stood erect she took naturally one of the attitudes in which court–painters represent queens and princesses; so that I found myself wondering whether, to draw out this accomplishment, I couldn't get the editor of the Cheapside to publish a really royal romance, "A Tale of Buckingham Palace." Sometimes however the real thing and the make– believe came into contact; by which I mean that Miss Churm, keeping an appointment or coming to make one on days when I had much work in hand, encountered her invidious rivals. The encounter was not on their part, for they noticed her no more than if she had been the housemaid; not from intentional loftiness, but simply because as yet, professionally, they didn't know how to fraternise, as I could imagine they would have liked—or at least that the Major would. They couldn't talk about the omnibus—they always walked; and they didn't know what else to try—she wasn't interested in good trains or cheap claret. Besides, they must have felt—in the air—that she was amused at them, secretly derisive of their ever knowing how. She wasn't a person to conceal the limits of her faith if she had had a chance to show them. On the other hand Mrs. Monarch didn't think her tidy; for why else did she take pains to say to me—it was going out of the way, for Mrs. Monarch—that she didn't like dirty women?

One day when my young lady happened to be present with my other sitters—she even dropped in, when it was convenient, for a chat—I asked her to be so good as to lend a hand in getting tea, a service with which she was familiar and which was one of a class that, living as I did in a small way, with slender domestic resources, I often appealed to my models to render. They liked to lay hands on my property, to break the sitting, and sometimes the china—it made them feel Bohemian. The next time I saw Miss Churm after this incident she surprised me greatly by making a scene about it—she accused me of having wished to humiliate her. She hadn't resented the outrage at the time, but had seemed obliging and amused, enjoying the comedy of asking Mrs. Monarch, who sat vague and silent, whether she would have cream and sugar, and putting an exaggerated simper into the question. She had tried intonations— as if she too wished to pass for the real thing—till I was afraid my other visitors would take offence.

Oh they were determined not to do this, and their touching patience was the measure of their great need. They would sit by the hour, uncomplaining, till I was ready to use them; they would come back on the chance of being wanted and would walk away cheerfully if it failed. I used to go to the door with them to see in what magnificent order they retreated. I tried to find other employment for them—I introduced them to several artists. But they didn't "take," for reasons I could appreciate, and I became rather anxiously aware that after such disappointments they fell back upon me with a heavier weight. They did me the honour to think me most their form. They weren't romantic enough for the painters, and in those days there were few serious workers in black–and–white.

Besides, they had an eye to the great job I had mentioned to them— they had secretly set their hearts on supplying the right essence for my pictorial vindication of our fine novelist. They knew that for this undertaking I should want no costume—effects, none of the frippery of past ages—that it was a case in which everything would be contemporary and satirical and presumably genteel. If I could work them into it their future would be assured, for the labour would of course be long and the occupation steady.

One day Mrs. Monarch came without her husband—she explained his absence by his having had to go to the City. While she sat there in her usual relaxed majesty there came at the door a knock which I immediately recognised as the subdued appeal of a model out of work. It was followed by the entrance of a young man whom I at once saw to be a foreigner and who proved in fact an Italian acquainted with no English word but my name, which he uttered in a way that made it seem to include all others. I hadn't then visited his country, nor was I proficient in his tongue; but as he was not so meanly constituted—what Italian is?—as to depend only on that member for expression he conveyed to me, in familiar but graceful mimicry, that he was in search of exactly the employment in which the lady before me was engaged. I was not struck with him at first, and while I continued to draw I dropped few signs of interest or encouragement. He stood his ground however—not importunately, but with a dumb dog–like fidelity in his eyes that amounted to innocent impudence, the manner of a devoted servant—he might have been in the house for years—unjustly suspected. Suddenly it struck me that this very attitude and expression made a picture; whereupon I told him to sit down and wait till I should be free. There was another picture in the way he obeyed me, and I observed as I worked that there were others still in the way he looked wonderingly, with his head thrown back, about the high studio. He might have been crossing himself in Saint Peter's. Before I finished I said to myself "The fellow's a bankrupt orange– monger, but a treasure."

When Mrs. Monarch withdrew he passed across the room like a flash to open the door for her, standing there with the rapt pure gaze of the young Dante spellbound by the young Beatrice. As I never insisted, in such situations, on the blankness of the British domestic, I reflected that he had the making of a servant—and I needed one, but couldn't pay him to be only that—as well as of a model; in short I resolved to adopt my bright adventurer if he would agree to officiate in the double capacity. He jumped at my offer, and in the event my rashness—for I had really known nothing about him—wasn't brought home to me. He proved a sympathetic though a desultory ministrant, and had in a wonderful degree the sentiment de la pose. It was uncultivated, instinctive, a part of the happy instinct that had guided him to my door and helped him to spell out my name on the card nailed to it. He had had no other introduction to me than a guess, from the shape of my high north window, seen outside, that my place was a studio and that as a studio it would contain an artist. He had wandered to England in search of fortune, like other itinerants, and had embarked, with a partner and a small green hand–cart, on the sale of penny ices. The ices had melted away and the partner had dissolved in their train. My young man wore tight yellow trousers with reddish stripes and his name was Oronte. He was sallow but fair, and when I put him into some old clothes of my own he looked like an Englishman. He was as good as Miss Churm, who could look, when requested, like an Italian.

CHAPTER IV

I thought Mrs. Monarch's face slightly convulsed when, on her coming back with her husband, she found Oronte installed. It was strange to have to recognise in a scrap of a lazzarone a competitor to her magnificent Major. It was she who scented danger first, for the Major was anecdotically unconscious. But Oronte gave us tea, with a hundred eager confusions—he had never been concerned in so queer a process—and I think she thought better of me for having at last an "establishment." They saw a couple of drawings that I had made of the establishment, and Mrs. Monarch hinted that it never would have struck her he had sat for them. "Now the drawings you make from US, they look exactly like us," she reminded me, smiling in triumph; and I recognised that this was indeed just their defect. When I drew the Monarchs I couldn't anyhow get away from them—get into the character I wanted to represent; and I hadn't the least desire my model should be discoverable in my picture. Miss Churm never was, and Mrs. Monarch thought I hid her, very properly, because she was vulgar; whereas if she was lost it was only as the dead who go to heaven are lost—in the gain of an angel the more.

By this time I had got a certain start with "Rutland Ramsay," the first novel in the great projected series; that is I had produced a dozen drawings, several with the help of the Major and his wife, and I had sent them in for approval. My understanding with the publishers as I have already hinted, had been that I was to be left to do my work, in this particular case, as I liked, with the whole book committed to me; but my connexion with the rest of the series was only contingent. There were moments when, frankly, it WAS a comfort to have the real thing under one's hand for there were characters in "Rutland Ramsay" that were very much like it. There were people presumably as erect as the Major and women of as good a fashion as Mrs. Monarch. There was a great deal of country–house life–treated, it is true, in a fine fanciful ironical generalised way—and there was a considerable implication of knickerbockers and kilts. There were certain things I had to settle at the outset; such things for instance as the exact appearance of the hero and the particular bloom and figure of the heroine. The author of course gave me a lead, but there was a margin for interpretation. I took the Monarchs into my confidence, I told them frankly what I was about, I mentioned my embarrassments and alternatives. "Oh take HIM!" Mrs. Monarch murmured sweetly, looking at her husband; and "What could you want better than my wife?" the Major inquired with the comfortable candour that now prevailed between us.

I wasn't obliged to answer these remarks—I was only obliged to place my sitters. I wasn't easy in mind, and I postponed a little timidly perhaps the solving of my question. The book was a large canvas, the other figures were numerous, and I worked off at first some of the episodes in which the hero and the heroine were not concerned. When once I had set THEM up I should have to stick to them—I couldn't make my young man seven feet high in one place and five feet nine in another. I inclined on the whole to the latter measurement, though the Major more than once reminded me that he looked about as young as any one. It was indeed quite possible to arrange him, for the figure, so that it would have been difficult to detect his age. After the spontaneous Oronte had been with me a month, and after I had given him to understand several times over that his native exuberance would presently constitute an insurmountable barrier to our further intercourse, I waked to a sense of his heroic capacity. He was only five feet seven, but the remaining inches were latent. I tried him almost secretly at first, for I was really rather afraid of the judgement my other models would pass on such a choice. If they regarded Miss Churm as little better than a snare what would they think of the representation by a person so little the real thing as an Italian street–vendor of a protagonist formed by a public school?

If I went a little in fear of them it wasn't because they bullied me, because they had got an oppressive foothold, but because in their really pathetic decorum and mysteriously permanent newness they counted on me so intensely. I was therefore very glad when Jack Hawley came home: he was always of such good counsel. He painted badly himself, but there was no one like him for putting his finger on the place. He had been absent from England for a year; he had been somewhere—I don't remember where—to get a fresh eye. I was in a good deal of dread of any such organ, but we were old friends; he had been away for months and a sense of emptiness was creeping into my life. I hadn't dodged a missile for a year.

He came back with a fresh eye, but with the same old black velvet blouse, and the first evening he spent in my studio we smoked cigarettes till the small hours. He had done no work himself, he had only got the eye; so the field was clear for the production of my little things. He wanted to see what I had produced for the Cheapside, but he was disappointed in the exhibition. That at least seemed the meaning of two or three comprehensive groans which, as he lounged on my big divan, his leg folded under him, looking at my latest drawings, issued from his lips with the smoke of the cigarette.

"What's the matter with you?" I asked.

"What's the matter with you?"

"Nothing save that I'm mystified."

"You are indeed. You're quite off the hinge. What's the meaning of this new fad?" And he tossed me, with visible irreverence, a drawing in which I happened to have depicted both my elegant models. I asked if he didn't think it good, and he replied that it struck him as execrable, given the sort of thing I had always represented myself to him as wishing to arrive at; but I let that pass—I was so anxious to see exactly what he meant. The two

34

figures in the picture looked colossal, but I supposed this was not what he meant, inasmuch as, for aught he knew to the contrary, I might have been trying for some such effect. I maintained that I was working exactly in the same way as when he last had done me the honour to tell me I might do something some day. "Well, there's a screw loose somewhere," he answered; "wait a bit and I'll discover it." I depended upon him to do so: where else was the fresh eye? But he produced at last nothing more luminous than "I don't know—I don't like your types." This was lame for a critic who had never consented to discuss with me anything but the question of execution, the direction of strokes and the mystery of values.

"In the drawings you've been looking at I think my types are very handsome."

"Oh they won't do!"

"I've been working with new models."

"I see you have. THEY won't do."

"Are you very sure of that?"

"Absolutely—they're stupid."

"You mean I am—for I ought to get round that."

"You can't—with such people. Who are they?"

I told him, so far as was necessary, and he concluded heartlessly: "Ce sont des gens qu'il faut mettre a la porte."

"You've never seen them; they're awfully good"—I flew to their defence.

"Not seen them? Why all this recent work of yours drops to pieces with them. It's all I want to see of them."

"No one else has said anything against it—the Cheapside people are pleased."

Some Short Stories

"Every one else is an ass, and the Cheapside people the biggest asses of all. Come, don't pretend at this time of day to have pretty illusions about the public, especially about publishers and editors. It's not for SUCH animals you work—it's for those who know, coloro che sanno; so keep straight for me if you can't keep straight for yourself. There was a certain sort of thing you used to try for—and a very good thing it was. But this twaddle isn't in it." When I talked with Hawley later about "Rutland Ramsay" and its possible successors he declared that I must get back into my boat again or I should go to the bottom. His voice in short was the voice of warning.

I noted the warning, but I didn't turn my friends out of doors. They bored me a good deal; but the very fact that they bored me admonished me not to sacrifice them—if there was anything to be done with them—simply to irritation. As I look back at this phase they seem to me to have pervaded my life not a little. I have a vision of them as most of the time in my studio, seated against the wall on an old velvet bench to be out of the way, and resembling the while a pair of patient courtiers in a royal antechamber. I'm convinced that during the coldest weeks of the winter they held their ground because it saved them fire. Their newness was losing its gloss, and it was impossible not to feel them objects of charity. Whenever Miss Churm arrived they went away, and after I was fairly launched in "Rutland Ramsay" Miss Churm arrived pretty often. They managed to express to me tacitly that they supposed I wanted her for the low life of the book, and I let them suppose it, since they had attempted to study the work—it was lying about the studio—without discovering that it dealt only with the highest circles. They had dipped into the most brilliant of our novelists without deciphering many passages. I still took an hour from them, now and again, in spite of Jack Hawley's warning: it would be time enough to dismiss them, if dismissal should be necessary, when the rigour of the season was over. Hawley had made their acquaintance– –he had met them at my fireside—and thought them a ridiculous pair. Learning that he was a painter they tried to approach him, to show him too that they were the real thing; but he looked at them across the big room, as if they were miles away: they were a compendium of everything he most objected to in the social system of his country. Such people as that, all convention and patent– leather, with ejaculations that stopped conversation, had no business in a studio. A studio was a place to learn to see, and how could you see through a pair of feather–beds?

The main inconvenience I suffered at their hands was that at first I was shy of letting it break upon them that my artful little servant had begun to sit to me for "Rutland Ramsay." They knew I had been odd enough—they were prepared by this time to allow oddity to artists—to pick a foreign vagabond out of the streets when I might have had a person with whiskers and credentials; but it was some time before they learned how high I rated his accomplishments. They found him in an attitude more than once, but they never doubted I was doing him as an organ–grinder. There were several things they never guessed, and one of them was that for a striking scene in the novel, in which a footman briefly figured, it occurred to me to make use of Major Monarch as the menial. I kept putting this off, I didn't like to ask him to don the livery— besides the difficulty of finding a livery to fit him. At last, one day late in the winter, when I was at work on the despised Oronte, who caught one's idea on the wing, and was in the glow of feeling myself go very straight, they came in, the Major and his wife, with their society laugh about nothing (there was less and less to laugh at); came in like country–callers—they always reminded me of that—who have walked across the park after church and are presently persuaded to stay to luncheon. Luncheon was over, but they could stay to tea—I knew they wanted it. The fit was on me, however, and I couldn't let my ardour cool and my work wait, with the fading daylight, while my model prepared it. So I asked Mrs. Monarch if she would mind laying it out—a request which for an instant brought all the blood to her face. Her eyes were on her husband's for a second, and some mute telegraphy passed between them. Their folly was over the next instant; his cheerful shrewdness put an end to it. So far from pitying their wounded pride, I must add, I was moved to give it as complete a lesson as I could. They bustled about together and got out the cups and saucers and made the kettle boil. I know they felt as if they were waiting on my servant, and when the tea was prepared I said: "He'll have a cup, please—he's tired." Mrs. Monarch brought him one where he stood, and he took it from her as if he had been a gentleman at a party squeezing a crush–hat with an elbow.

Then it came over me that she had made a great effort for me—made it with a kind of nobleness—and that I owed her a compensation. Each time I saw her after this I wondered what the compensation could be. I couldn't go on doing the wrong thing to oblige them. Oh it WAS the wrong thing, the stamp of the work for which they sat—Hawley was not the only person to say it now. I sent in a large number of the drawings I had made for "Rutland Ramsay," and I received a warning that was more to the point than Hawley's. The artistic adviser of the house for which I was working was of opinion that many of my illustrations were not what had been looked for. Most of these illustrations were the subjects in which the Monarchs had figured. Without going into the question of what HAD been looked for, I had to face the fact that at this rate I shouldn't get the other books to do. I hurled myself in despair on Miss Churm—I put her through all her paces. I not only adopted Oronte publicly as my hero, but one morning when the Major looked in to see if I didn't require him to finish a Cheapside figure for which he had begun to sit the week before, I told him I had changed my mind—I'd do the drawing from my man. At this my visitor turned pale and stood looking at me. "Is HE your idea of an English gentleman?" he asked.

I was disappointed, I was nervous, I wanted to get on with my work; so. I replied with irritation: "Oh my dear Major—I can't be ruined for YOU!"

It was a horrid speech, but he stood another moment—after which, without a word, he quitted the studio. I drew a long breath, for I said to myself that I shouldn't see him again. I hadn't told—him definitely that I was in danger of having my work rejected, but I was vexed at his not having felt the catastrophe in the air, read with me the moral of our fruitless collaboration, the lesson that in the deceptive atmosphere of art even the highest respectability may fail of being plastic.

I didn't owe my friends money, but I did see them again. They reappeared together three days later, and, given all the other facts, there was something tragic in that one. It was a clear proof they could find nothing else in life to do. They had threshed the matter out in a dismal conference—they had digested the bad news that they were not in for the series. If they weren't useful to me even for the Cheapside their function seemed difficult to determine, and I could only judge at first that they had come, forgivingly, decorously, to take a last leave. This made me rejoice in secret that I had little leisure for a scene; for I had placed both my other models in position together and I was pegging away at a drawing from which I hoped to derive glory. It had been suggested by the passage in —which Rutland Ramsay, drawing up a chair to Artemisia's piano−stool, says extraordinary things to her while she ostensibly fingers out a difficult piece of music. I had done Miss Churm at the piano before—it was an attitude in which she knew how to take on an absolutely poetic grace. I wished the two figures to "compose" together with intensity, and my little Italian had entered perfectly into my conception. The pair were vividly before me, the piano had been pulled out; it was a charming show of blended youth and murmured love, which I had only to catch and keep. My visitors stood and looked at it, and I was friendly to them over my shoulder.

They made no response, but I was used to silent company and went on with my work, only a little disconcerted—even though exhilarated by the sense that this was at least the

38

ideal thing—at not having got rid of them after all. Presently I heard Mrs. Monarch's sweet voice beside or rather above me: "I wish her hair were a little better done." I looked up and she was staring with a strange fixedness at Miss Churm, whose back was turned to her. "Do you mind my just touching it?" she went on—a question which made me spring up for an instant as with the instinctive fear that she might do the young lady a harm. But she quieted me with a glance I shall never forget—I confess I should like to have been able to paint that—and went for a moment to my model. She spoke to her softly, laying a hand on her shoulder and bending over her; and as the girl, understanding, gratefully assented, she disposed her rough curls, with a few quick passes, in such a way as to make Miss Churm's head twice as charming. It was one of the most heroic personal services I've ever seen rendered. Then Mrs. Monarch turned away with a low sigh and, looking about her as if for something to do, stooped to the floor with a noble humility and picked up a dirty rag that had dropped out of my paint–box.

The Major meanwhile had also been looking for something to do, and, wandering to the other end of the studio, saw before him my breakfast–things neglected, unremoved. "I say, can't I be useful HERE?" he called out to me with an irrepressible quaver. I assented with a laugh that I fear was awkward, and for the next ten minutes, while I worked, I heard the light clatter of china and the tinkle of spoons and glass. Mrs. Monarch assisted her husband— they washed up my crockery, they put it away. They wandered off into my little scullery, and I afterwards found that they had cleaned my knives and that my slender stock of plate had an unprecedented surface. When it came over me, the latent eloquence of what they were doing, I confess that my drawing was blurred for a moment—the picture swam. They had accepted their failure, but they couldn't accept their fate. They had bowed their heads in bewilderment to the perverse and cruel law in virtue of which the real thing could be so much less precious than the unreal; but they didn't want to starve. If my servants were my models, then my models might be my servants. They would reverse the parts—the others would sit for the ladies and gentlemen and THEY would do the work. They would still be in the studio—it was an intense dumb appeal to me not to turn them out. "Take us on," they wanted to say—"we'll do ANYTHING."

My pencil dropped from my hand; my sitting was spoiled and I got rid of my sitters, who were also evidently rather mystified and awestruck. Then, alone with the Major and his wife I had a most uncomfortable moment. He put their prayer into a single sentence: "I say, you know—just let US do for you, can't you?" I couldn't— it was dreadful to see them emptying my slops; but I pretended I could, to oblige them, for about a week. Then I gave them a sum of money to go away, and I never saw them again. I obtained the remaining books, but my friend Hawley repeats that Major and Mrs. Monarch did me a permanent harm, got me into false ways. If it be true I'm content to have paid the price—for the memory.

THE STORY OF IT

CHAPTER I

The weather had turned so much worse that the rest of the day was certainly lost. The wind had risen and the storm gathered force; they gave from time to time a thump at the firm windows and dashed even against those protected by the verandah their vicious splotches of rain. Beyond the lawn, beyond the cliff, the great wet brush of the sky dipped deep into the sea. But the lawn, already vivid with the touch of May, showed a violence of watered green; the budding shrubs and trees repeated the note as they tossed their thick masses, and the cold troubled light, filling the pretty saloon, marked the spring afternoon as sufficiently young. The two ladies seated there in silence could pursue without difficulty—as well as, clearly, without interruption—their respective tasks; a confidence expressed, when the noise of the wind allowed it to be heard, by the sharp scratch of Mrs. Dyott's pen at the table where she was busy with letters.

Her visitor, settled on a small sofa that, with a palm-tree, a screen, a stool, a stand, a bowl of flowers and three photographs in silver frames, had been arranged near the light wood-fire as a choice "corner"—Maud Blessingbourne, her guest, turned audibly, though at intervals neither brief nor regular, the leaves of a book covered in lemon-coloured paper and not yet despoiled of a certain fresh crispness. This effect of the volume, for the eye, would have made it, as presumably the newest French novel—and evidently, from the attitude of the reader, "good"—consort happily with the special tone of the room, a consistent air of selection and suppression, one of the finer aesthetic evolutions. If Mrs. Dyott was fond of ancient French furniture and distinctly difficult about it, her inmates could be fond—with whatever critical cocks of charming dark-braided heads over slender sloping shoulders—of modern French authors. Nothing bad passed for half an hour— nothing at least, to be exact, but that each of the companions occasionally and covertly intermitted her pursuit in such a manner as to ascertain the degree of absorption of the other without turning round. What their silence was charged with therefore was not only a sense of the weather, but a sense, so to speak, of its own nature. Maud Blessingbourne, when she lowered her book into her lap, closed her eyes with a conscious patience that seemed to say she waited; but it was nevertheless she who at last made the movement representing a snap of their tension. She got up and stood by the fire, into which she looked a minute; then came round and approached the window as if to see what was really going on. At this Mrs. Dyott wrote with refreshed intensity. Her little pile of letters had grown, and if a look of determination was compatible with her fair and slightly faded beauty the habit of attending to her business could always keep pace with any excursion of her thought. Yet she was the first who spoke.

"I trust your book has been interesting."

"Well enough; a little mild."

A louder throb of the tempest had blurred the sound of the words. "A little wild?"

"Dear no—timid and tame; unless I've quite lost my sense."

"Perhaps you have," Mrs. Dyott placidly suggested—"reading so many."

Her companion made a motion of feigned despair. "Ah you take away my courage for going to my room, as I was just meaning to, for another."

"Another French one?"

"I'm afraid."

"Do you carry them by the dozen—?"

"Into innocent British homes?" Maud tried to remember. "I believe I brought three—seeing them in a shop−window as I passed through town. It never rains but it pours! But I've already read two."

"And are they the only ones you do read?"

"French ones?" Maud considered. "Oh no. D'Annunzio."

"And what's that?" Mrs. Dyott asked as she affixed a stamp.

"Oh you dear thing!" Her friend was amused, yet almost showed pity. "I know you don't read," Maud went on; "but why should you? YOU live!"

"Yes—wretchedly enough," Mrs. Dyott returned, getting her letters together. She left her place, holding them as a neat achieved handful, and came over to the fire, while Mrs. Blessingbourne turned once more to the window, where she was met by another flurry.

Maud spoke then as if moved only by the elements. "Do you expect him through all this?"

Mrs. Dyott just waited, and it had the effect, indescribably, of making everything that had gone before seem to have led up to the question. This effect was even deepened by the way she then said "Whom do you mean?"

"Why I thought you mentioned at luncheon that Colonel Voyt was to walk over. Surely he can't."

"Do you care very much?" Mrs. Dyott asked.

Her friend now hesitated. "It depends on what you call 'much.' If you mean should I like to see him—then certainly."

"Well, my dear, I think he understands you're here."

"So that as he evidently isn't coming," Maud laughed, "it's particularly flattering! Or rather," she added, giving up the prospect again, "it would be, I think, quite extraordinarily flattering if he did. Except that of course," she threw in, "he might come partly for you."

"'Partly' is charming. Thank you for 'partly.' If you ARE going upstairs, will you kindly," Mrs Dyott pursued, "put these into the box as you pass?"

The younger woman, taking the little pile of letters, considered them with envy. "Nine! You ARE good. You're always a living reproach!"

Mrs. Dyott gave a sigh. "I don't do it on purpose. The only thing, this afternoon," she went on, reverting to the other question, "would be their not having come down."

"And as to that you don't know."

"No—I don't know." But she caught even as she spoke a rat–tat–tat of the knocker, which struck her as a sign. "Ah there!"

"Then I go." And Maud whisked out.

Mrs. Dyott, left alone, moved with an air of selection to the window, and it was as so stationed, gazing out at the wild weather, that the visitor, whose delay to appear spoke of the wiping of boots and the disposal of drenched mackintosh and cap, finally found her. He was tall lean fine, with little in him, on the whole, to confirm the titular in the "Colonel Voyt" by which he was announced. But he had left the army, so that his reputation for gallantry mainly depended now on his fighting Liberalism in the House of Commons. Even these facts, however, his aspect scantily matched; partly, no doubt, because he looked, as was usually said, un–English. His black hair, cropped close, was lightly powdered with silver, and his dense glossy beard, that of an emir or a caliph, and grown for civil reasons, repeated its handsome colour and its somewhat foreign effect. His nose had a strong and shapely arch, and the dark grey of his eyes was tinted with blue. It had been said of him—in relation to these signs—that he would have struck you as a Jew had he not, in spite of his nose, struck you so much as an Irishman. Neither responsibility could in fact have been fixed upon him, and just now, at all events, he was only a pleasant weather–washed wind–battered Briton, who brought in from a struggle with the elements that he appeared quite to have enjoyed a certain amount of unremoved mud and an unusual quantity of easy expression. It was exactly the silence ensuing on the retreat of the servant and the closed door that marked between him and his hostess the degree of this ease. They met, as it were, twice: the first time while the servant was there and the second as soon as he was not. The difference was great between the two encounters, though we must add in justice to the second that its marks were at first mainly negative. This communion consisted only in their having drawn each other for a minute as close as possible—as possible, that is, with no help but the full clasp of hands.

43

Thus they were mutually held, and the closeness was at any rate such that, for a little, though it took account of dangers, it did without words. When words presently came the pair were talking by the fire and she had rung for tea. He had by this time asked if the note he had despatched to her after breakfast had been safely delivered.

"Yes, before luncheon. But I'm always in a state when—except for some extraordinary reason—you send such things by hand. I knew, without it, that you had come. It never fails. I'm sure when you're there—I'm sure when you're not."

He wiped, before the glass, his wet moustache. "I see. But this morning I had an impulse."

"It was beautiful. But they make me as uneasy, sometimes, your impulses, as if they were calculations; make me wonder what you have in reserve."

"Because when small children are too awfully good they die? Well, I AM a small child compared to you—but I'm not dead yet. I cling to life."

He had covered her with his smile, but she continued grave. "I'm not half so much afraid when you're nasty."

"Thank you! What then did you do," he asked, "with my note?"

"You deserve that I should have spread it out on my dressing–table– –or left it, better still, in Maud Blessingbourne's room."

He wondered while he laughed. "Oh but what does SHE deserve?"

It was her gravity that continued to answer. "Yes—it would probably kill her."

"She believes so in you?"

"She believes so in YOU. So don't be TOO nice to her."

He was still looking, in the chimney–glass, at the state of his beard—brushing from it, with his handkerchief, the traces of wind and wet. "If she also then prefers me when I'm nasty it seems to me I ought to satisfy her. Shall I now at any rate see her?"

"She's so like a pea on a pan over the possibility of it that she's pulling herself together in her room."

"Oh then we must try and keep her together. But why, graceful tender, pretty too—quite or almost as she is —doesn't she re– marry?"

Mrs. Dyott appeared—and as if the first time—to look for the reason. "Because she likes too many men."

It kept up his spirits. "And how many MAY a lady like—?"

"In order not to like any of them too much? Ah that, you know, I never found out—and it's too late now. When," she presently pursued, "did you last see her?"

He really had to think. "Would it have been since last November or so?—somewhere or other where we spent three days."

"Oh at Surredge? I know all about that. I thought you also met afterwards."

He had again to recall. "So we did! Wouldn't it have been somewhere at Christmas? But it wasn't by arrangement!" he laughed, giving with his forefinger a little pleasant nick to his hostess's chin. Then as if something in the way she received this attention put him back to his question of a moment before: "Have you kept my note?"

She held him with her pretty eyes. "Do you want it back?"

"Ah don't speak as if I did take things—!"

She dropped her gaze to the fire. "No, you don't; not even the hard things a really generous nature often would." She quitted, however, as if to forget that, the chimney–place. "I put it THERE!"

"You've burnt it? Good!" It made him easier, but he noticed the next moment on a table the lemon–coloured volume left there by Mrs. Blessingbourne, and, taking it up for a look, immediately put it down. "You might while you were about it have burnt that too."

"You've read it?"

"Dear yes. And you?"

"No," said Mrs. Dyott; "it wasn't for me Maud brought it."

It pulled her visitor up. "Mrs. Blessingbourne brought it?"

"For such a day as this." But she wondered. "How you look! Is it so awful?"

"Oh like his others." Something had occurred to him; his thought was already far. "Does she know?"

"Know what?"

"Why anything."

But the door opened too soon for Mrs. Dyott, who could only murmur quickly—"Take care!"

CHAPTER II

It was in fact Mrs. Blessingbourne, who had under her arm the book she had gone up for—a pair of covers showing this time a pretty, a candid blue. She was followed next minute by the servant, who brought in tea, the consumption of which, with the passage of greetings, inquiries and other light civilities between the two visitors, occupied a quarter of an hour. Mrs. Dyott meanwhile, as a contribution to so much amenity, mentioned to Maud that her fellow guest wished to scold her for the books she read—a statement met by this friend with the remark that he must first be sure about them. But as soon as he had picked up the new, the blue volume he broke out into a frank "Dear, dear!"

"Have you read that too?" Mrs. Dyott inquired. "How much you'll have to talk over together! The other one," she explained to him, "Maud speaks of as terribly tame."

"Ah I must have that out with her! You don't feel the extraordinary force of the fellow?" Voyt went on to Mrs. Blessingbourne.

And so, round the hearth, they talked—talked soon, while they warmed their toes, with zest enough to make it seem as happy a chance as any of the quieter opportunities their imprisonment might have involved. Mrs. Blessingbourne did feel, it then appeared, the force of the fellow, but she had her reserves and reactions, in which Voyt was much interested. Mrs. Dyott rather detached herself, mainly gazing, as she leaned back, at the fire; she intervened, however, enough to relieve Maud of the sense of being listened to. That sense, with Maud, was too apt to convey that one was listened to for a fool. "Yes, when I read a novel I mostly read a French one," she had said to Voyt in answer to a question about her usual practice; "for I seem with it to get hold more of the real thing—to get more life for my money. Only I'm not so infatuated with them but that sometimes for months and months on end I don't read any fiction at all."

The two books were now together beside them. "Then when you begin again you read a mass?"

"Dear no. I only keep up with three or four authors."

He laughed at this over the cigarette he had been allowed to light. "I like your 'keeping up,' and keeping up in particular with 'authors.'"

"One must keep up with somebody," Mrs. Dyott threw off.

"I daresay I'm ridiculous," Mrs. Blessingbourne conceded without heeding it; "but that's the way we express ourselves in my part of the country."

"I only alluded," said Voyt, "to the tremendous conscience of your sex. It's more than mine can keep up with. You take everything too hard. But if you can't read the novel of British and American manufacture, heaven knows I'm at one with you. It seems really to show our sense of life as the sense of puppies and kittens."

"Well," Maud more patiently returned, "I'm told all sorts of people are now doing wonderful things; but somehow I remain outside."

"Ah it's THEY, it's our poor twangers and twaddlers who remain outside. They pick up a living in the street. And who indeed would want them in?"

Mrs. Blessingbourne seemed unable to say, and yet at the same time to have her idea. The subject, in truth, she evidently found, was not so easy to handle. "People lend me things, and I try; but at the end of fifty pages—"

"There you are! Yes—heaven help us!"

"But what I mean," she went on, "isn't that I don't get woefully weary of the eternal French thing. What's THEIR sense of life?"

"Ah voila!" Mrs. Dyott softly sounded.

"Oh but it IS one; you can make it out," Voyt promptly declared. "They do what they feel, and they feel more things than we. They strike so many more notes, and with so different a hand. When it comes to any account of a relation say between a man and a woman—I mean an intimate or a curious or a suggestive one—where are we compared to them? They don't exhaust the subject, no doubt," he admitted; "but we don't touch it, don't even skim it. It's as if we denied its existence, its possibility. You'll doubtless tell me, however," he went on, "that as all such relations ARE for us at the most much simpler we can only have all round less to say about them."

She met this imputation with the quickest amusement. "I beg your pardon. I don't think I shall tell you anything of the sort. I don't know that I even agree with your premiss."

"About such relations?" He looked agreeably surprised. "You think we make them larger?—or subtler?"

Mrs. Blessingbourne leaned back, not looking, like Mrs. Dyott, at the fire, but at the ceiling. "I don't know what I think."

"It's not that she doesn't know," Mrs. Dyott remarked. "It's only that she doesn't say."

But Voyt had this time no eye for their hostess. For a moment he watched Maud. "It sticks out of you, you know, that you've yourself written something. Haven't you—and

48

published? I've a notion I could read YOU."

"When I do publish," she said without moving, "you'll be the last one I shall tell. I HAVE," she went on, "a lovely subject, but it would take an amount of treatment—!"

"Tell us then at least what it is."

At this she again met his eyes. "Oh to tell it would be to express it, and that's just what I can't do. What I meant to say just now," she added, "was that the French, to my sense, give us only again and again, for ever and ever, the same couple. There they are once more, as one has had them to satiety, in that yellow thing, and there I shall certainly again find them in the blue."

"Then why do you keep reading about them?" Mrs. Dyott demanded.

Maud cast about. "I don't!" she sighed. "At all events, I shan't any more. I give it up."

"You've been looking for something, I judge," said Colonel Voyt, "that you're not likely to find. It doesn't exist."

"What is it?" Mrs. Dyott desired to know.

"I never look," Maud remarked, "for anything but an interest."

"Naturally. But your interest," Voyt replied, "is in something different from life."

"Ah not a bit! I LOVE life in art, though I hate it anywhere else. It's the poverty of the life those people show, and the awful bounders, of both sexes, that they represent."

"Oh now we have you!" her interlocutor laughed. "To me, when all's said and done, they seem to be—as near as art can come—in the truth of the truth. It can only take what life gives it, though it certainly may be a pity that that isn't better. Your complaint of their monotony is a complaint of their conditions. When you say we get always the same couple what do you mean but that we get always the same passion? Of course we do!" Voyt pursued. "If what you're looking for is another, that's what you won't anywhere find."

Maud for a while said nothing, and Mrs. Dyott seemed to wait. "Well, I suppose I'm looking, more than anything else, for a decent woman."

"Oh then you mustn't look for her in pictures of passion. That's not her element nor her whereabouts."

Mrs. Blessingbourne weighed the objection. "Does it not depend on what you mean by passion?"

"I think I can mean only one thing: the enemy to behaviour."

"Oh I can imagine passions that are on the contrary friends to it."

Her fellow–guest thought. "Doesn't it depend perhaps on what you mean by behaviour?"

"Dear no. Behaviour's just behaviour—the most definite thing in the world."

"Then what do you mean by the 'interest' you just now spoke of? The picture of that definite thing?"

"Yes—call it that. Women aren't ALWAYS vicious, even when they're—"

"When they're what?" Voyt pressed.

"When they're unhappy. They can be unhappy and good."

"That one doesn't for a moment deny. But can they be 'good' and interesting?"

"That must be Maud's subject!" Mrs. Dyott interposed. "To show a woman who IS. I'm afraid, my dear," she continued, "you could only show yourself."

"You'd show then the most beautiful specimen conceivable"—and Voyt addressed himself to Maud. "But doesn't it prove that life is, against your contention, more interesting than art? Life you embellish and elevate; but art would find itself able to do nothing with you, and, on such impossible terms, would ruin you."

50

The colour in her faint consciousness gave beauty to her stare. "'Ruin' me?"

"He means," Mrs. Dyott again indicated, "that you'd ruin 'art.'"

"Without on the other hand"—Voyt seemed to assent—"its giving at all a coherent impression of you."

"She wants her romance cheap!" said Mrs. Dyott.

"Oh no—I should be willing to pay for it. I don't see why the romance—since you give it that name—should be all, as the French inveterately make it, for the women who are bad."

"Oh they pay for it!" said Mrs. Dyott.

"DO they?"

"So at least"—Mrs. Dyott a little corrected herself—"one has gathered (for I don't read your books, you know!) that they're usually shown as doing."

Maud wondered, but looking at Voyt, "They're shown often, no doubt, as paying for their badness. But are they shown as paying for their romance?"

"My dear lady," said Voyt, "their romance is their badness. There isn't any other. It's a hard law, if you will, and a strange, but goodness has to go without that luxury. Isn't to BE good just exactly, all round, to go without?" He put it before her kindly and clearly—regretfully too, as if he were sorry the truth should be so sad. He and she, his pleasant eyes seemed to say, would, had they had the making of it, have made it better. "One has heard it before—at least I have; one has heard your question put. But always, when put to a mind not merely muddled, for an inevitable answer. 'Why don't you, cher monsieur, give us the drama of virtue?' 'Because, chere madame, the high privilege of virtue is precisely to avoid drama.' The adventures of the honest lady? The honest lady hasn't, can't possibly have, adventures."

Mrs. Blessingbourne only met his eyes at first, smiling with some intensity. "Doesn't it depend a little on what you call adventures?"

51

"My poor Maud," said Mrs. Dyott as if in compassion for sophistry so simple, "adventures are just adventures. That's all you can make of them!"

But her friend talked for their companion and as if without hearing. "Doesn't it depend a good deal on what you call drama?" Maud spoke as one who had already thought it out. "Doesn't it depend on what you call romance?"

Her listener gave these arguments his very best attention. "Of course you may call things anything you like—speak of them as one thing and mean quite another. But why should it depend on anything? Behind these words we use—the adventure, the novel, the drama, the romance, the situation, in short, as we most comprehensively say—behind them all stands the same sharp fact which they all in their different ways represent."

"Precisely!" Mrs. Dyott was full of approval.

Maud however was full of vagueness. "What great fact?"

"The fact of a relation. The adventure's a relation; the relation's an adventure. The romance, the novel, the drama are the picture of one. The subject the novelist treats is the rise, the formation, the development, the climax and for the most part the decline of one. And what is the honest lady doing on that side of the town?"

Mrs. Dyott was more pointed. "She doesn't so much as FORM a relation."

But Maud bore up. "Doesn't it depend again on what you call a relation?"

"Oh," said Mrs. Dyott, "if a gentleman picks up her pocket- handkerchief—"

"Ah even that's one," their friend laughed, "if she has thrown it to him. We can only deal with one that is one."

"Surely," Maud replied. "But if it's an innocent one—"

"Doesn't it depend a good deal," Mrs. Dyott asked, "on what you call innocent?"

"You mean that the adventures of innocence have so often been the material of fiction? Yes," Voyt replied; "that's exactly what the bored reader complains of. He has asked for bread and been given a stone. What is it but, with absolute directness, a question of interest or, as people say, of the story? What's a situation undeveloped but a subject lost? If a relation stops, where's the story? If it doesn't stop, where's the innocence? It seems to me you must choose. It would be very pretty if it were otherwise, but that's how we flounder. Art is our flounderings shown."

Mrs. Blessingbourne—and with an air of deference scarce supported perhaps by its sketchiness—kept her deep eyes on this definition. "But sometimes we flounder out."

It immediately touched in Colonel Voyt the spring of a genial derision. "That's just where I expected YOU would! One always sees it come."

"He has, you notice," Mrs. Dyott parenthesised to Maud, "seen it come so often I; and he has always waited for it and met it."

"Met it, dear lady, simply enough! It's the old story, Mrs. Blessingbourne. The relation's innocent that the heroine gets out of. The book's innocent that's the story of her getting out. But what the devil—in the name of innocence—was she doing IN?"

Mrs. Dyott promptly echoed the question. "You have to be in, you know, to GET out. So there you are already with your relation. It's the end of your goodness."

"And the beginning," said Voyt, "of your play!"

"Aren't they all, for that matter, even the worst," Mrs. Dyott pursued, "supposed SOME time or other to get out? But if meanwhile they've been in, however briefly, long enough to adorn a tale?"

"They've been in long enough to point a moral. That is to point ours!" With which, and as if a sudden flush of warmer light had moved him, Colonel Voyt got up. The veil of the storm had parted over a great red sunset.

Mrs. Dyott also was on her feet, and they stood before his charming antagonist, who, with eyes lowered and a somewhat fixed smile, had not moved.

"We've spoiled her subject!" the elder lady sighed.

"Well," said Voyt, "it's better to spoil an artist's subject than to spoil his reputation. I mean," he explained to Maud with his indulgent manner, "his appearance of knowing what he has got hold of, for that, in the last resort, is his happiness."

She slowly rose at this, facing him with an aspect as handsomely mild as his own. "You can't spoil my happiness."

He held her hand an instant as he took leave. "I wish I could add to it!"

CHAPTER III

When he had quitted them and Mrs. Dyott had candidly asked if her friend had found him rude or crude, Maud replied—though not immediately—that she had feared showing only too much how charming she found him. But if Mrs. Dyott took this it was to weigh the sense. "How could you show it too much?"

"Because I always feel that that's my only way of showing anything. It's absurd, if you like," Mrs. Blessingbourne pursued, "but I never know, in such intense discussions, what strange impression I may give."

Her companion looked amused. "Was it intense?"

"_I_ was," Maud frankly confessed.

"Then it's a pity you were so wrong. Colonel Voyt, you know, is right." Mrs. Blessingbourne at this gave one of the slow soft silent headshakes to which she often resorted and which, mostly accompanied by the light of cheer, had somehow, in spite of the small obstinacy that smiled in them, a special grace. With this grace, for a moment, her friend, looking her up and down, appeared impressed, yet not too much so to take the next minute a decision. "Oh my dear, I'm sorry to differ from any one so lovely—for you're awfully beautiful to–night, and your frock's the very nicest I've ever seen you wear. But he's as right as he can be."

Maud repeated her motion. "Not so right, at all events as he thinks he is. Or perhaps I can say," she went on, after an instant, "that I'm not so wrong. I do know a little what I'm talking about."

Mrs. Dyott continued to study her. "You ARE vexed. You naturally don't like it—such destruction."

"Destruction?"

"Of your illusion."

"I HAVE no illusion. If I had moreover it wouldn't be destroyed. I have on the whole, I think, my little decency."

Mrs. Dyott stared. "Let us grant it for argument. What, then?"

"Well, I've also my little drama."

"An attachment ?"

"An attachment."

"That you shouldn't have?"

"That I shouldn't have."

"A passion?"

"A passion."

"Shared?"

"Ah thank goodness, no!"

Mrs. Dyott continued to gaze. "The object's unaware—?"

"Utterly."

Mrs. Dyott turned it over. "Are you sure?"

"Sure."

"That's what you call your decency? But isn't it," Mrs. Dyott asked, "rather his?"

"Dear no. It's only his good fortune."

Mrs. Dyott laughed. "But yours, darling—your good fortune: where does THAT come in?"

"Why, in my sense of the romance of it."

"The romance of what? Of his not knowing?"

"Of my not wanting him to. If I did"—Maud had touchingly worked it out—"where would be my honesty?"

The inquiry, for an instant, held her friend, yet only, it seemed, for a stupefaction that was almost amusement. "Can you want or not want as you like? Where in the world, if you don't want, is your romance?"

Mrs. Blessingbourne still wore her smile, and she now, with a light gesture that matched it, just touched the region of her heart. "There!"

Her companion admiringly marvelled. "A lovely place for it, no doubt!—but not quite a place, that I can see, to make the sentiment a relation."

"Why not? What more is required for a relation for me?"

"Oh all sorts of things, I should say! And many more, added to those, to make it one for the person you mention."

"Ah that I don't pretend it either should be or CAN be. I only speak for myself."

This was said in a manner that made Mrs. Dyott, with a visible mixture of impressions, suddenly turn away. She indulged in a vague movement or two, as if to look for something; then again found herself near her friend, on whom with the same abruptness, in fact with a strange sharpness, she conferred a kiss that might have represented either her tribute to exalted consistency or her idea of a graceful close of the discussion. "You deserve that one should speak FOR you!"

Her companion looked cheerful and secure. "How CAN you without knowing—?"

"Oh by guessing! It's not—?"

But that was as far as Mrs. Dyott could get. "It's not," said Maud, "any one you've ever seen."

"Ah then I give you up!"

And Mrs. Dyott conformed for the rest of Maud's stay to the spirit of this speech. It was made on a Saturday night, and Mrs. Blessingbourne remained till the Wednesday following, an interval during which, as the return of fine weather was confirmed by the Sunday, the two ladies found a wider range of action. There were drives to be taken, calls made, objects of interest seen at a distance; with the effect of much easy talk and still more easy silence. There had been a question of Colonel Voyt's probable return on the Sunday, but the whole time passed without a sign from him, and it was merely mentioned by Mrs. Dyott, in explanation, that he must have been suddenly called, as he was so liable to be, to town. That this in fact was what had happened he made clear to her on Thursday afternoon, when, walking over again late, he found her alone. The consequence of his Sunday letters had been his taking, that day, the 4.15. Mrs. Voyt had gone back on Thursday, and he now, to settle on the spot the question of a piece of work begun at his place, had rushed down for a few hours in anticipation of the usual collective move for the week's end. He was to go up again by the late train, and had to count a little—a fact accepted by his hostess with the hard pliancy of practice—his present happy moments. Too few as these were, however, he found time to make of her an inquiry or two not directly bearing on their situation. The first was a recall of the question for which Mrs. Blessingbourne's entrance on the previous Saturday had arrested her answer. Had that lady the idea of anything between them?

"No. I'm sure. There's one idea she has got," Mrs. Dyott went on; "but it's quite different and not so very wonderful."

"What then is it?"

"Well, that she's herself in love."

Voyt showed his interest. "You mean she told you?"

"I got it out of her."

He showed his amusement. "Poor thing! And with whom?"

"With you."

His surprise, if the distinction might be made, was less than his wonder. "You got that out of her too?"

"No—it remains in. Which is much the best way for it. For you to know it would be to end it."

He looked rather cheerfully at sea. "Is that then why you tell me?"

"I mean for her to know you know it. Therefore it's in your interest not to let her."

"I see," Voyt after a moment returned. "Your real calculation is that my interest will be sacrificed to my vanity—so that, if your other idea is just, the flame will in fact, and thanks to her morbid conscience, expire by her taking fright at seeing me so pleased. But I promise you," he declared, "that she shan't see it. So there you are!" She kept her eyes on him and had evidently to admit after a little that there she was. Distinct as he had made the case, however, he wasn't yet quite satisfied. "Why are you so sure I'm the man?"

"From the way she denies you."

"You put it to her?"

"Straight. If you hadn't been she'd of course have confessed to you—to keep me in the dark about the real one."

Poor Voyt laughed out again. "Oh you dear souls!"

"Besides," his companion pursued, "I wasn't in want of that evidence."

"Then what other had you?"

"Her state before you came—which was what made me ask you how much you had seen her. And her state after it," Mrs. Dyott added. "And her state," she wound up, "while you were here."

"But her state while I was here was charming."

"Charming. That's just what I say."

She said it in a tone that placed the matter in its right light—a light in which they appeared kindly, quite tenderly, to watch Maud wander away into space with her lovely head bent under a theory rather too big for it. Voyt's last word, however, was that there was just enough in it—in the theory—for them to allow that she had not shown herself, on the occasion of their talk, wholly bereft of sense. Her consciousness, if they let it alone—as they of course after this mercifully must—WAS, in the last analysis, a kind of shy romance. Not a romance like their own, a thing to make the fortune of any author up to the mark—one who should have the invention or who COULD have the courage; but a small scared starved subjective satisfaction that would do her no harm and nobody else any good. Who but a duffer—he stuck to his contention—would see the shadow of a "story" in it?

FLICKERBRIDGE

CHAPTER I

Frank Granger had arrived from Paris to paint a portrait—an order given him, as a young compatriot with a future, whose early work would some day have a price, by a lady from

Some Short Stories

New York, a friend of his own people and also, as it happened, of Addie's, the young woman to whom it was publicly both affirmed and denied that he was engaged. Other young women in Paris—fellow-members there of the little tight transpontine world of art-study—professed to know that the pair had "several times" over renewed their fond understanding. This, however, was their own affair; the last phase of the relation, the last time of the times, had passed into vagueness; there was perhaps even an impression that if they were inscrutable to their friends they were not wholly crystalline to each other and themselves. What had occurred for Granger at all events in connexion with the portrait was that Mrs. Bracken, his intending model, whose return to America was at hand, had suddenly been called to London by her husband, occupied there with pressing business, but had yet desired that her displacement should not interrupt her sittings. The young man, at her request, had followed her to England and profited by all she could give him, making shift with a small studio lent him by a London painter whom he had known and liked a few years before in the French atelier that then cradled, and that continued to cradle, so many of their kind.

The British capital was a strange grey world to him, where people walked, in more ways than one, by a dim light; but he was happily of such a turn that the impression, just as it came, could nowhere ever fail him, and even the worst of these things was almost as much an occupation—putting it only at that—as the best. Mrs. Bracken moreover passed him on, and while the darkness ebbed a little in the April days he found himself consolingly committed to a couple of fresh subjects. This cut him out work for more than another month, but meanwhile, as he said, he saw a lot—a lot that, with frequency and with much expression, he wrote about to Addie. She also wrote to her absent friend, but in briefer snatches, a meagreness to her reasons for which he had long since assented. She had other play for her pen as well as, fortunately, other remuneration; a regular correspondence for a "prominent Boston paper," fitful connexions with public sheets perhaps also in cases fitful, and a mind above all engrossed at times, to the exclusion of everything else, with the study of the short story. This last was what she had mainly come out to go into, two or three years after he had found himself engulfed in the mystery of Carolus. She was indeed, on her own deep sea, more engulfed than he had ever been, and he had grown to accept the sense that, for progress too, she sailed under more canvas. It hadn't been particularly present to him till now that he had in the least got on, but the way in which Addie had—and evidently still more would—was the theme, as it were, of every tongue. She had thirty short stories out and nine descriptive articles. His three or four portraits of fat American ladies—they were all fat, all ladies and all American— were a poor show compared with these triumphs; especially as Addie had begun to throw out that it was about time they should go home. It kept perpetually coming up in Paris, in the transpontine world, that, as the phrase was, America had grown more interesting since they left. Addie was attentive to the rumour, and, as full of conscience as she was of taste, of patriotism as of curiosity, had often put it to him frankly, with what he, who was of New York, recognised as her New England emphasis: "I'm not sure, you know, that we do REAL justice to our country." Granger felt he would do it on the day—if the day ever came—he should irrevocably marry her. No other country could possibly have produced her.

CHAPTER II

But meanwhile it befell that, in London, he was stricken with influenza and with subsequent sorrow. The attack was short but sharp—had it lasted Addie would certainly have come to his aid; most of a blight really in its secondary stage. The good ladies his sitters—the ladies with the frizzled hair, with the diamond earrings, with the chins tending to the massive—left for him, at the door of his lodgings, flowers, soup and love, so that with their assistance he pulled through; but his convalescence was slow and his weakness out of proportion to the muffled shock. He came out, but he went about lame; it tired him to paint—he felt as if he had been ill three months. He strolled in Kensington Gardens when he should have been at work; he sat long on penny chairs and helplessly mused and mooned. Addie desired him to return to Paris, but there were chances under his hand that he felt he had just wit enough left not to relinquish. He would have gone for a week to the sea—he would have gone to Brighton; but Mrs. Bracken had to be finished—Mrs. Bracken was so soon to sail. He just managed to finish her in time—the day before the date fixed for his breaking ground on a greater business still, the circumvallation of Mrs. Dunn. Mrs. Dunn duly waited on him, and he sat down before her, feeling, however, ere he rose, that he must take a long breath before the attack. While asking himself that night, therefore, where he should best replenish his lungs he received from Addie, who had had from Mrs. Bracken a poor report of him, a communication which, besides being of sudden and startling interest, applied directly to his case.

His friend wrote to him under the lively emotion of having from one day to another become aware of a new relative, an ancient cousin, a sequestered gentlewoman, the sole survival of "the English branch of the family," still resident, at Flickerbridge, in the "old family home," and with whom, that he might immediately betake himself to so auspicious a quarter for change of air, she had already done what was proper to place him, as she said, in touch. What came of it all, to be brief, was that Granger found himself so placed almost as he read: he was in touch with Miss Wenham of Flickerbridge, to the extent of being in correspondence with her, before twenty–four hours had sped. And on the second day he was in the train, settled for a five–hours' run to the door of this amiable woman who had so abruptly and kindly taken him on trust and of whom but yesterday he had never so much as heard. This was an oddity—the whole incident was—of which, in the corner of his compartment, as he proceeded, he had time to take the size. But the surprise, the incongruity, as he felt, could but deepen as he went. It was a sufficiently queer note, in the light, or the absence of it, of his late experience, that so complex a product as Addie should have ANY simple insular tie; but it was a queerer note still that she should have had one so long only to remain unprofitably unconscious of it. Not to have done something with it, used it, worked it, talked about it at least, and perhaps even written—these things, at the rate she moved, represented a loss of opportunity under which as he saw her, she was peculiarly formed to wince. She was at any rate, it was clear, doing something with it now; using it, working it, certainly, already talking—and, yes, quite possibly writing—about it. She was in short smartly making up what she had missed, and he could take such comfort from his own action as he had been helped to by the rest of the facts, succinctly reported from Paris on the very morning of his start.

It was the singular story of a sharp split—in a good English house—that dated now from years back. A worthy Briton, of the best middling stock, had, during the fourth decade of the century, as a very young man, in Dresden, whither he had been despatched to qualify in German for a stool in an uncle's counting–house, met, admired, wooed and won an American girl, of due attractions, domiciled at that period with her parents and a sister, who was also attractive, in the Saxon capital. He had married her, taken her to England, and there, after some years of harmony and happiness, lost her. The sister in question had, after her death, come to him and to his young child on a visit, the effect of which, between the pair, eventually defined itself as a sentiment that was not to be resisted. The bereaved husband, yielding to a new attachment and a new response, and finding a new union thus prescribed, had yet been forced to reckon with the unaccommodating law of the land. Encompassed with frowns in his own country, however, marriages of this particular type were wreathed in smiles in his sister's–in–law, so that his remedy was not forbidden. Choosing between two allegiances he had let the one go that seemed the least close, and had in brief transplanted his possibilities to an easier air. The knot was tied for

62

the couple in New York, where, to protect the legitimacy of such other children as might come to them, they settled and prospered. Children came, and one of the daughters, growing up and marrying in her turn, was, if Frank rightly followed, the mother of his own Addie, who had been deprived of the knowledge of her indeed, in childhood, by death, and been brought up, though without undue tension, by a stepmother— —a character breaking out thus anew.

The breach produced in England by the invidious action, as it was there held, of the girl's grandfather, had not failed to widen—all the more that nothing had been done on the American side to close it. Frigidity had settled, and hostility had been arrested only by indifference. Darkness therefore had fortunately supervened, and a cousinship completely divided. On either side of the impassable gulf, of the impenetrable curtain, each branch had put forth its leaves—a foliage failing, in the American quarter, it was distinct enough to Granger, of no sign or symptom of climate and environment. The graft in New York had taken, and Addie was a vivid, an unmistakable flower. At Flickerbridge, or wherever, on the other hand, strange to say, the parent stem had had a fortune comparatively meagre. Fortune, it was true, in the vulgarest sense, had attended neither party. Addie's immediate belongings were as poor as they were numerous, and he gathered that Miss Wenham's pretensions to wealth were not so marked as to expose the claim of kinship to the imputation of motive. To this lady's single identity the original stock had at all events dwindled, and our young man was properly warned that he would find her shy and solitary. What was singular was that in these conditions she should desire, she should endure, to receive him. But that was all another story, lucid enough when mastered. He kept Addie's letters, exceptionally copious, in his lap; he conned them at intervals; he held the threads.

He looked out between whiles at the pleasant English land, an April aquarelle washed in with wondrous breadth. He knew the French thing, he knew the American, but he had known nothing of this. He saw it already as the remarkable Miss Wenham's setting. The doctor's daughter at Flickerbridge, with nippers on her nose, a palette on her thumb and innocence in her heart, had been the miraculous link. She had become aware even there, in our world of wonders, that the current fashion for young women so equipped was to enter the Parisian lists. Addie had accordingly chanced upon her, on the slopes of Montparnasse, as one of the English girls in one of the thorough–going sets. They had met in some easy collocation and had fallen upon common ground; after which the young woman, restored to Flickerbridge for an interlude and retailing there her adventures and impressions, had mentioned to Miss Wenham who had known and protected her from babyhood, that that lady's own name of Adelaide was, as well as the surname conjoined with it, borne, to her knowledge, in Paris, by an extraordinary American specimen. She had then recrossed the Channel with a wonderful message, a courteous challenge, to her friend's duplicate, who had in turn granted through her every satisfaction. The duplicate had in other words bravely let Miss Wenham know exactly who she was. Miss Wenham, in whose personal tradition the flame of resentment appeared to have been reduced by time to the palest ashes—for whom indeed the story of the great schism was now but a legend only needing a little less dimness to make it romantic—Miss Wenham had promptly responded by a letter fragrant with the hope that old threads might be taken up. It was a relationship that they must puzzle out together, and she had earnestly sounded the other party to it on the subject of a possible visit. Addie had met her with a definite promise; she would come soon, she would come when free, she would come in July; but meanwhile she sent her deputy. Frank asked himself by what name she had described, by what character introduced him to Flickerbridge. He mainly felt on the whole as if he were going there to find out if he were engaged to her. He was at sea really now as to which of the various views Addie herself took of it. To Miss Wenham she must definitely have taken one, and perhaps Miss Wenham would reveal it. This expectation was in fact his excuse for a possible indiscretion.

CHAPTER III

He was indeed to learn on arrival to what he had been committed; but that was for a while so much a part of his first general impression that the particular truth took time to detach itself, the first general impression demanding verily all his faculties of response. He almost felt for a day or two the victim of a practical joke, a gross abuse of confidence. He had presented himself with the moderate amount of flutter involved in a sense of due preparation; but he had then found that, however primed with prefaces and prompted with hints, he hadn't been prepared at all. How COULD he be, he asked himself, for anything so foreign to his experience, so alien to his proper world, so little to be preconceived in the sharp north light of the newest impressionism, and yet so recognised after all in the event, so noted and tasted and assimilated? It was a case he would scarce have known how to describe—could doubtless have described best with a full clean brush, supplemented by a play of gesture; for it was always his habit to see an occasion, of whatever kind, primarily as a picture, so that he might get it, as he was wont to say, so that he might keep it, well together. He had been treated of a sudden, in this adventure, to one of the sweetest fairest coolest impressions of his life—one moreover visibly complete and homogeneous from the start. Oh it was THERE, if that was all one wanted of a thing! It was so "there" that, as had befallen him in Italy, in Spain, confronted at last, in dusky side–chapel or rich museum, with great things dreamed of or with greater ones unexpectedly presented, he had held his breath for fear of breaking the spell; had almost, from the quick impulse to respect, to prolong, lowered his voice and moved on tiptoe. Supreme beauty suddenly revealed is apt to strike us as a possible illusion playing with our desire—instant freedom with it to strike us as a possible rashness.

This fortunately, however—and the more so as his freedom for the time quite left him—didn't prevent his hostess, the evening of his advent and while the vision was new, from being exactly as queer and rare and IMPAYABLE, as improbable, as impossible, as delightful at the eight o'clock dinner—she appeared to keep these immense hours—as she had overwhelmingly been at the five o'clock tea. She was in the most natural way in the world one of the oddest apparitions, but that the particular means to such an end COULD be natural was an inference difficult to make. He failed in fact to make it for a couple of days; but then—though then only—he made it with confidence. By this time indeed he was sure of everything, luckily including himself. If we compare his impression, with slight extravagance, to some of the greatest he had ever received, this is simply because the image before him was so rounded and stamped. It expressed with pure perfection, it exhausted its character. It was so absolutely and so unconsciously what it was. He had been floated by the strangest of chances out of the rushing stream into a clear still backwater—a deep and quiet pool in which objects were sharply mirrored. He had hitherto in life known nothing that was old except a few statues and pictures; but here everything was old, was immemorial, and nothing so much so as the very freshness itself. Vaguely to have supposed there were such nooks in the world had done little enough, he now saw, to temper the glare of their opposites. It was the fine touches that counted, and these had to be seen to be believed.

Miss Wenham, fifty–five years of age and unappeasably timid, unaccountably strange, had, on her reduced scale, an almost Gothic grotesqueness; but the final effect of one's sense of it was an amenity that accompanied one's steps like wafted gratitude. More flurried, more spasmodic, more apologetic, more completely at a loss at one moment and more precipitately abounding at another, he had never before in all his days seen any maiden lady; yet for no maiden lady he had ever seen had he so promptly conceived a private enthusiasm. Her eyes protruded, her chin receded and her nose carried on in conversation a queer little independent motion. She wore on the top of her head an upright circular cap that made her resemble a caryatid disburdened, and on other parts of her person strange combinations of colours, stuffs, shapes, of metal, mineral and plant. The tones of her voice rose and fell, her facial convulsions, whether tending—one could scarce make out—to expression or REpression, succeeded each other by a law of their own; she was embarrassed at nothing and at everything, frightened at everything and at nothing, and she approached objects, subjects, the simplest questions and answers and the whole material of intercourse, either with the indirectness of terror or with the violence of despair. These things, none the less, her refinements of oddity and intensities of custom, her betrayal at once of conventions and simplicities, of ease and of agony, her roundabout retarded suggestions and perceptions, still permitted her to strike her guest as irresistibly charming. He didn't know what to call it; she was a fruit of time. She had a queer distinction. She had been expensively produced and there would be a good deal more of her to come.

The result of the whole quality of her welcome, at any rate, was that the first evening, in his room, before going to bed, he relieved his mind in a letter to Addie, which, if space allowed us to embody it in our text, would usefully perform the office of a "plate." It would enable us to present ourselves as profusely illustrated. But the process of reproduction, as we say, costs. He wished his friend to know how grandly their affair turned out. She had put him in the way of something absolutely special—an old house untouched, untouchable, indescribable, an old corner such as one didn't believe existed, and the holy calm of which made the chatter of studios, the smell of paint, the slang of critics, the whole sense and sound of Paris, come back as so many signs of a huge monkey–cage. He moved about, restless, while he wrote; he lighted cigarettes and, nervous and suddenly scrupulous, put them out again; the night was mild and one of the windows of his large high room, which stood over the garden, was up. He lost himself in the things about him, in the type of the room, the last century with not a chair moved, not a point stretched. He hung over the objects and ornaments, blissfully few and adorably good, perfect pieces all, and never one, for a change, French. The scene was as rare as some fine old print with the best bits down in the corners. Old books and old pictures, allusions remembered and aspects conjectured, reappeared to him; he knew not what anxious islanders had been trying for in their backward hunt for the homely. But the homely at Flickerbridge was all style, even as style at the same time was mere honesty. The larger, the smaller past—he scarce knew which to call it—was at all events so hushed to sleep round him as he wrote that he had almost a bad conscience about having come. How one might love it, but how one might spoil it! To look at it too hard was positively to make it conscious, and to make it conscious was positively to wake it up. Its only safety, of a truth, was to be left still to sleep—to sleep in its large fair chambers and under its high clean canopies.

He added thus restlessly a line to his letter, maundered round the room again, noted and fingered something else, and then, dropping on the old flowered sofa, sustained by the tight cubes of its cushions, yielded afresh to the cigarette, hesitated, stared, wrote a few words more. He wanted Addie to know, that was what he most felt, unless he perhaps felt, more how much she herself would want to. Yes, what he supremely saw was all that Addie would make of it. Up to his neck in it there he fairly turned cold at the sense of suppressed opportunity, of the outrage of privation that his correspondent would retrospectively and, as he even divined with a vague shudder, almost vindictively nurse. Well, what had happened was that the acquaintance had been kept for her, like a packet enveloped and sealed for delivery, till her attention was free. He saw her there, heard her and felt her—felt how she would feel and how she would, as she usually said, "rave." Some of her young compatriots called it "yell," and in the reference itself, alas! illustrated their meaning. She would understand the place at any rate, down to the ground; there wasn't the slightest doubt of that. Her sense of it would be exactly like his own, and he could see, in anticipation, just the terms of recognition and rapture in which she would abound. He knew just what she would call quaint, just what she would call bland, just what she would call weird, just what she would call wild. She would take it all in with an intelligence much more fitted than his own, in fact, to deal with what he supposed he must regard as its literary relations. She would have read the long-winded obsolete memoirs and novels that both the figures and the setting ought clearly to remind one of; she would know about the past generations—the lumbering country magnates and their turbaned wives and round-eyed daughters, who, in other days, had treated the ruddy sturdy tradeless town,—the solid square houses and wide walled gardens, the streets to-day all grass and gossip, as the scene of a local "season." She would have warrant for the assemblies, dinners, deep potations; for the smoked sconces in the dusky parlours; for the long muddy century of family coaches, "holsters," highwaymen. She would put a finger in short, just as he had done, on the vital spot—the rich humility of the whole thing, the fact that neither Flickerbridge in general nor Miss Wenham in particular, nor anything nor any one concerned, had a suspicion of their characters and their merit. Addie and he would have to come to let in light.

He let it in then, little by little, before going to bed, through the eight or ten pages he addressed to her; assured her that it was the happiest case in the world, a little picture—yet full of "style" too—absolutely composed and transmitted, with tradition, and tradition only, in every stroke, tradition still noiselessly breathing and visibly flushing, marking strange hours in the tall mahogany clocks that were never wound up and that yet audibly ticked on. All the elements, he was sure he should see, would hang together with a charm, presenting his hostess—a strange iridescent fish for the glazed exposure of an aquarium—as afloat in her native medium. He left his letter open on the table, but, looking it over next morning, felt of a sudden indisposed to send it. He would keep it to add more, for there would be more to know; yet when three days had elapsed he still had not sent it. He sent instead, after delay, a much briefer report, which he was moved to make different and, for some reason, less vivid. Meanwhile he learned from Miss Wenham how Addie had introduced him. It took time to arrive with her at that point, but after the Rubicon was crossed they went far afield.

CHAPTER IV

"Oh yes, she said you were engaged to her. That was why—since I HAD broken out—she thought I might like to see you; as I assure you I've been so delighted to. But AREN'T you?" the good lady asked as if she saw in his face some ground for doubt.

"Assuredly—if she says so. It may seem very odd to you, but I haven't known, and yet I've felt that, being nothing whatever to you directly, I need some warrant for consenting thus to be thrust on you. We WERE," the young man explained, "engaged a year ago; but since then (if you don't mind my telling you such things; I feel now as if I could tell you anything!) I haven't quite known how I stand. It hasn't seemed we were in a position to marry. Things are better now, but I haven't quite known how she'd see them. They were so bad six months ago that I understood her, I thought, as breaking off. I haven't broken; I've only accepted, for the time—because men must be easy with women—being treated as 'the best of friends.' Well, I try to be. I wouldn't have come here if I hadn't been. I thought it would be charming for her to know you—when I heard from her the extraordinary way you had dawned upon her; and charming therefore if I could help her to it. And if I'm helping you to know HER," he went on, "isn't that charming too?"

"Oh I so want to!" Miss Wenham murmured in her unpractical impersonal way. "You're so different!" she wistfully declared.

"It's YOU, if I may respectfully, ecstatically say so, who are different. That's the point of it all. I'm not sure that anything so terrible really ought to happen to you as to know us."

"Well," said Miss Wenham, "I do know you a little by this time, don't I? And I don't find it terrible. It's a delightful change for me."

"Oh I'm not sure you ought to have a delightful change!"

"Why not—if you do?"

"Ah I can bear it. I'm not sure you can. I'm too bad to spoil—I AM spoiled. I'm nobody, in short; I'm nothing. I've no type. You're ALL type. It has taken delicious long years of security and monotony to produce you. You fit your frame with a perfection only equalled by the perfection with which your frame fits you. So this admirable old house, all time–softened white within and time–faded red without, so everything that surrounds you here and that has, by some extraordinary mercy, escaped the inevitable fate of exploitation: so it all, I say, is the sort of thing that, were it the least bit to fall to pieces, could never, ah never more be put together again. I have, dear Miss Wenham," Granger went on, happy himself in his extravagance, which was yet all sincere, and happier still in her deep but altogether pleased mystification—"I've found, do you know, just the thing one has ever heard of that you most resemble. You're the Sleeping Beauty in the Wood."

He still had no compunction when he heard her bewilderedly sigh: "Oh you're too delightfully droll!"

"No, I only put thing's just as they are, and as I've also learned a little, thank heaven, to see them—which isn't, I quite agree with you, at all what any one does. You're in the deep doze of the spell that has held you for long years, and it would be a shame, a crime, to wake you up. Indeed I already feel with a thousand scruples that I'm giving you the fatal shake. I say it even though it makes me sound a little as if I thought myself the fairy prince."

She gazed at him with her queerest kindest look, which he was getting used to in spite of a faint fear, at the back of his head, of the strange things that sometimes occurred when lonely ladies, however mature, began to look at interesting young men from over the seas as if the young men desired to flirt. "It's so wonderful," she said, "that you should be so very odd and yet so very good–natured." Well, it all came to the same thing—it was so wonderful that SHE should be so simple and yet so little of a bore. He accepted with gratitude the theory of his languor—which moreover was real enough and partly perhaps why he was so sensitive; he let himself go as a convalescent, let her insist on the weakness always left by fever. It helped him to gain time, to preserve the spell even while he talked of breaking it; saw him through slow strolls and soft sessions, long gossips, fitful hopeless questions—there was so much more to tell than, by any contortion, she COULD—and explanations addressed gallantly and patiently to her understanding, but not, by good fortune, really reaching it. They were perfectly at cross–purposes, and it was the better, and they wandered together in the silver haze with all communication blurred.

When they sat in the sun in her formal garden he quite knew how little even the tenderest consideration failed to disguise his treating her as the most exquisite of curiosities. The term of comparison most present to him was that of some obsolete musical instrument. The old–time order of her mind and her air had the stillness of a painted spinet that was duly dusted, gently rubbed, but never tuned nor played on. Her opinions were like dried rose– leaves; her attitudes like British sculpture; her voice what he imagined of the possible tone of the old gilded silver–stringed harp in one of the corners of the drawing–room. The lonely little decencies and modest dignities of her life, the fine grain of its conservatism, the innocence of its ignorance, all its monotony of stupidity and salubrity, its cold dulness and dim brightness, were there before him. Meanwhile within him strange things took place. It was literally true that his impression began again, after a lull, to make him nervous and anxious, and for reasons peculiarly confused, almost grotesquely mingled, or at least comically sharp. He was distinctly an agitation and a new taste—that he could see; and he saw quite as much therefore the excitement she already drew from the vision of Addie, an image intensified by the sense of closer kinship and presented to her, clearly, with various erratic enhancements, by her friend the doctor's daughter. At the end of a few days he said to her: "Do you know she wants to come without waiting any longer? She wants to come while I'm here. I received this morning her letter proposing it, but I've been thinking it over and have waited to speak to you. The thing is, you see, that if she writes to YOU proposing it—"

"Oh I shall be so particularly glad!"

CHAPTER V

They were as usual in the garden, and it hadn't yet been so present to him that if he were only a happy cad there would be a good way to protect her. As she wouldn't hear of his being yet beyond precautions she had gone into the house for a particular shawl that was just the thing for his knees, and, blinking in the watery sunshine, had come back with it across the fine little lawn. He was neither fatuous nor asinine, but he had almost to put it to himself as a small task to resist the sense of his absurd advantage with her. It filled him with horror and awkwardness, made him think of he didn't know what, recalled something of Maupassant's— the smitten "Miss Harriet" and her tragic fate. There was a preposterous possibility—yes, he held the strings quite in his hands—of keeping the treasure for himself. That was the art of life—what the real artist would consistently do. He would close the door on his impression, treat it as a private museum. He would see that he could lounge and linger there, live with wonderful things there, lie up there to rest and refit. For himself he was sure that after a little he should be able to paint there—do things in a key he had never thought of before. When she brought him the rug he took it from her and made her sit down on the bench and resume her knitting; then, passing behind her with a laugh, he placed it over her own shoulders; after which he moved to and fro before her, his hands in his pockets and his cigarette in his teeth. He was ashamed of the cigarette—a villainous false note; but she allowed, liked, begged him to smoke, and what he said to her on it, in one of the pleasantries she benevolently missed, was that he did so for fear of doing worse. That only showed how the end was really in sight. "I dare say it will strike you as quite awful, what I'm going to say to you, but I can't help it. I speak out of the depths of my respect for you. It will seem to you horrid disloyalty to poor Addie. Yes—there we are; there _I_ am at least in my naked monstrosity." He stopped and looked at her till she might have been almost frightened. "Don't let her come. Tell her not to. I've tried to prevent it, but she suspects."

The poor woman wondered. "Suspects?"

"Well, I drew it, in writing to her, on reflexion, as mild as I could—having been visited in the watches of the night by the instinct of what might happen. Something told me to keep back my first letter—in which, under the first impression, I myself rashly 'raved'; and I concocted instead of it an insincere and guarded report. But guarded as I was I clearly didn't keep you 'down,' as we say, enough. The wonder of your colour—daub you over with grey as I might—must have come through and told the tale. She scents battle from afar—by which I mean she scents 'quaintness.' But keep her off. It's hideous, what I'm saying—but I owe it to you. I owe it to the world. She'll kill you."

"You mean I shan't get on with her?"

"Oh fatally! See how _I_ have. And see how you have with ME. She's intelligent, moreover, remarkably pretty, remarkably good. And she'll adore you."

"Well then?"

"Why that will be just how she'll do for you."

"Oh I can hold my own!" said Miss Wenham with the headshake of a horse making his sleigh–bells rattle in frosty air.

"Ah but you can't hold hers! She'll rave about you. She'll write about you. You're Niagara before the first white traveller—and you know, or rather you can't know, what Niagara became AFTER that gentleman. Addie will have discovered Niagara. She'll understand you in perfection; she'll feel you down to the ground; not a delicate shade of you will she lose or let any one else lose. You'll be too weird for words, but the words will nevertheless come. You'll be too exactly the real thing and be left too utterly just as you are, and all Addie's friends and all Addie's editors and contributors and readers will cross the Atlantic and flock to Flickerbridge just in order so—unanimously, universally, vociferously—to leave you. You'll be in the magazines with illustrations; you'll be in the papers with headings; you'll be everywhere with everything. You don't understand—you think you do, but you don't. Heaven forbid you SHOULD understand! That's just your beauty—your 'sleeping' beauty. But you needn't. You can take me on trust. Don't have her. Give as a pretext, as a reason, anything in the world you like. Lie to her—scare her away. I'll go away and give you up—I'll sacrifice everything myself." Granger pursued his exhortation, convincing himself more and more. "If I saw my way out, my way completely through, I'D pile up some fabric of fiction for her—I should only want to be sure of its not tumbling down. One would have, you see, to keep the thing up. But I'd throw dust in her eyes. I'd tell her you don't do at all—that you're not in fact a desirable acquaintance. I'd tell her you're vulgar, improper, scandalous; I'd tell her you're mercenary, designing, dangerous; I'd tell her the only safe course is immediately to let you drop. I'd thus surround you with an impenetrable legend of conscientious misrepresentation, a circle of pious fraud, and all the while privately keep you for myself."

She had listened to him as if he were a band of music and she herself a small shy garden–party. "I shouldn't like you to go away. I shouldn't in the least like you not to come again."

"Ah there it is!" he replied. "How can I come again if Addie ruins you?"

"But how will she ruin me—even if she does what you say? I know I'm too old to change and really much too queer to please in any of the extraordinary ways you speak of. If it's a question of quizzing me I don't think my cousin, or any one else, will have quite the hand for it that YOU seem to have. So that if YOU haven't ruined me—!"

"But I HAVE—that's just the point!" Granger insisted. "I've undermined you at least. I've left after all terribly little for Addie to do."

She laughed in clear tones. "Well then, we'll admit that you've done everything but frighten me."

He looked at her with surpassing gloom. "No—that again is one of the most dreadful features. You'll positively like it—what's to come. You'll be caught up in a chariot of fire like the prophet— wasn't there, was there one?—of old. That's exactly why—if one could but have done it—you'd have been to be kept ignorant and helpless. There's something or other in Latin that says it's the finest things that change the most easily for the worse. You already enjoy your dishonour and revel in your shame. It's too late—you're lost!"

CHAPTER VI

All this was as pleasant a manner of passing the time as any other, for it didn't prevent his old–world corner from closing round him more entirely, nor stand in the way of his making out from day to day some new source as well as some new effect of its virtue. He was really scared at moments at some of the liberties he took in talk—at finding himself so familiar; for the great note of the place was just that a certain modern ease had never crossed its threshold, that quick intimacies and quick oblivions were a stranger to its air. It had known in all its days no rude, no loud invasion. Serenely unconscious of most contemporary things, it had been so of nothing so much as of the diffused social practice of running in and out. Granger held his breath on occasions to think how Addie would run. There were moments when, more than at others, for some reason, he heard her step on the staircase and her cry in the hall. If he nevertheless played freely with the idea with which we have shown him as occupied it wasn't that in all palpable ways he didn't sacrifice so far as mortally possible to stillness. He only hovered, ever so lightly, to take up again his thread. She wouldn't hear of his leaving her, of his being in the least fit again, as she said, to travel. She spoke of the journey to London— —which was in fact a matter of many hours—as an experiment fraught with lurking complications. He added then day to day, yet only hereby, as he reminded her, giving other complications a larger chance to multiply. He kept it before her, when there was nothing else to do, that she must consider; after which he had his times of fear that she perhaps really would make for him this sacrifice.

He knew she had written again to Paris, and knew he must himself again write—a situation abounding for each in the elements of a plight. If he stayed so long why then he wasn't better, and if he wasn't better Addie might take it into her head—! They must make it clear that he WAS better, so that, suspicious, alarmed at what was kept from her, she shouldn't suddenly present herself to nurse him. If he was better, however, why did he stay so long? If he stayed only for the attraction the sense of the attraction might be contagious. This was what finally grew clearest for him, so that he had for his mild disciple hours of still sharper prophecy. It consorted with his fancy to represent to her that their young friend had been by this time unsparingly warned; but nothing could be plainer than that this was ineffectual so long as he himself resisted the ordeal. To plead that he remained because he was too weak to move was only to throw themselves back on the other horn of their dilemma. If he was too weak to move Addie would bring him her strength—of which, when she got there, she would give them specimens enough. One morning he broke out at breakfast with an intimate conviction. They'd see that she was actually starting— they'd receive a wire by noon. They didn't receive it, but by his theory the portent was only the stronger. It had moreover its grave as well as its gay side, since Granger's paradox and pleasantry were only the method most open to him of conveying what he felt. He literally heard the knell sound, and in expressing this to Miss Wenham with the conversational freedom that seemed best to pay his way he the more vividly faced the contingency. He could never return, and though he announced it with a despair that did what might be to make it pass as a joke, he saw how, whether or no she at last understood, she quite at last believed him. On this, to his knowledge, she wrote again to Addie, and the contents of her letter excited his curiosity. But that sentiment, though not assuaged, quite dropped when, the day after, in the evening, she let him know she had had a telegram an hour before.

"She comes Thursday."

He showed not the least surprise. It was the deep calm of the fatalist. It HAD to be. "I must leave you then to—morrow."

She looked, on this, as he had never seen her; it would have been hard to say whether what showed in her face was the last failure to follow or the first effort to meet. "And really not to come back?"

"Never, never, dear lady. Why should I come back? You can never be again what you HAVE been. I shall have seen the last of you."

"Oh!" she touchingly urged.

"Yes, for I should next find you simply brought to self- consciousness. You'll be exactly what you are, I charitably admit— —nothing more or less, nothing different. But you'll be it all in a different way. We live in an age of prodigious machinery, all organised to a single end. That end is publicity—a publicity as ferocious as the appetite of a cannibal. The thing therefore is not to have any illusions—fondly to flatter yourself in a muddled moment that the cannibal will spare you. He spares nobody. He spares nothing. It will be all right. You'll have a lovely time. You'll be only just a public character—blown about the world 'for all you're worth,' and proclaimed 'for all you're worth' on the house—tops. It will be for THAT, mind, I quite recognise—because Addie is superior—as well as for all you aren't. So good—bye."

He remained however till the next day, and noted at intervals the different stages of their friend's journey; the hour, this time, she would really have started, the hour she'd reach Dover, the hour she'd get to town, where she'd alight at Mrs. Dunn's. Perhaps she'd bring Mrs. Dunn, for Mrs. Dunn would swell the chorus. At the last, on the morrow, as if in anticipation of this stillness settled between them: he became as silent as his hostess. But before he went she brought out shyly and anxiously, as an appeal, the question that for hours had clearly been giving her thought. "Do you meet her then to—night in London?"

"Dear no. In what position am I, alas! to do that? When can I EVER meet her again?" He had turned it all over. "If I could meet Addie after this, you know, I could meet YOU. And if I do meet Addie," he lucidly pursued, "what will happen by the same stroke is that I SHALL meet you. And that's just what I've explained to you I dread."

"You mean she and I will be inseparable?"

He hesitated. "I mean she'll tell me all about you. I can hear her and her ravings now."

She gave again—and it was infinitely sad—her little whinnying laugh. "Oh but if what you say is true you'll know."

"Ah but Addie won't! Won't, I mean, know that _I_ know—or at least won't believe it. Won't believe that any one knows. Such," he added with a strange smothered sigh, "is Addie. Do you know," he wound up, "that what, after all, has most definitely happened is that you've made me see her as I've never done before?"

She blinked and gasped, she wondered and despaired. "Oh no, it will be YOU. I've had nothing to do with it. Everything's all you!"

But for all it mattered now! "You'll see," he said, "that she's charming. I shall go for to—night to Oxford. I shall almost cross her on the way."

"Then if she's charming what am I to tell her from you in explanation of such strange behaviour as your flying away just as she arrives?"

"Ah you needn't mind about that—you needn't tell her anything."

She fixed him as if as never again. "It's none of my business, of course I feel; but isn't it a little cruel if you're engaged?"

Granger gave a laugh almost as odd as one of her own. "Oh you've cost me that!"—and he put out his hand to her.

She wondered while she took it. "Cost you—?"

"We're not engaged. Good–bye."

MRS. MEDWIN

CHAPTER I

"Well, we ARE a pair!" the poor lady's visitor broke out to her at the end of her explanation in a manner disconcerting enough. The poor lady was Miss Cutter, who lived in South Audley Street, where she had an "upper half" so concise that it had to pass boldly for convenient; and her visitor was her half–brother, whom she hadn't seen for three years. She was remarkable for a maturity of which every symptom might have been observed to be admirably controlled, had not a tendency to stoutness just affirmed its independence. Her present, no doubt, insisted too much on her past, but with the excuse, sufficiently valid, that she must certainly once have been prettier. She was clearly not contented with once—she wished to be prettier again. She neglected nothing that could produce that illusion, and, being both fair and fat, dressed almost wholly in black. When she added a little colour it was not, at any rate, to her drapery. Her small rooms had the peculiarity that everything they contained appeared to testify with vividness to her position in society, quite as if they had been furnished by the bounty of admiring friends. They were adorned indeed almost exclusively with objects that nobody buys, as had more than once been remarked by spectators of her own sex, for herself, and would have been luxurious if luxury consisted mainly in photographic portraits slashed across with signatures, in baskets of flowers beribboned with the cards of passing compatriots, and in a neat collection of red volumes, blue volumes, alphabetical volumes, aids to London lucidity, of every sort, devoted to addresses and engagements. To be in Miss Cutter's tiny drawing–room, in short, even with Miss Cutter alone—should you by any chance have found her so—was somehow to be in the world and in a crowd. It was like an agency— it bristled with particulars.

This was what the tall lean loose gentleman lounging there before her might have appeared to read in the suggestive scene over which, while she talked to him, his eyes moved without haste and without rest. "Oh come, Mamie!" he occasionally threw off; and the words were evidently connected with the impression thus absorbed. His comparative youth spoke of waste even as her positive—her too positive—spoke of economy. There was only one thing, that is, to make up in him for everything he had lost, though it was distinct enough indeed that this thing might sometimes serve. It consisted in the perfection of an indifference, an indifference at the present moment directed to the plea—a plea of inability, of pure destitution—with which his sister had met him. Yet it had even now a wider embrace, took in quite sufficiently all consequences of queerness, confessed in advance to the false note that, in such a setting, he almost excruciatingly constituted. He cared as little that he looked at moments all his impudence as that he looked all his shabbiness, all his cleverness, all his history. These different things were written in him—in his premature baldness, his seamed strained face, the lapse from bravery of his long tawny moustache; above all in his easy friendly universally acquainted eye, so much too sociable for mere conversation. What possible relation with him could be natural enough to meet it? He wore a scant rough Inverness cape and a pair of black trousers, wanting in substance and marked with the sheen of time, that had presumably once served for evening use. He spoke with the slowness helplessly permitted to Americans—as something too slow to be stopped—and he repeated that he found himself associated with Miss Cutter in a harmony calling for wonder. She had been telling him not only that she couldn't possibly give him ten pounds, but that his unexpected arrival, should he insist on being much in view, might seriously interfere with arrangements necessary to her own maintenance; on which he had begun by replying that he of course knew she had long ago spent her money, but that he looked to her now exactly because she had, without the aid of that convenience, mastered the art of life.

"I'd really go away with a fiver, my dear, if you'd only tell me how you do it. It's no use saying only, as you've always said, that 'people are very kind to you.' What the devil are they kind to you FOR?"

"Well, one reason is precisely that no particular inconvenience has hitherto been supposed to attach to me. I'm just what I am," said Mamie Cutter; "nothing less and nothing more. It's awkward to have to explain to you, which moreover I really needn't in the least. I'm clever and amusing and charming." She was uneasy and even frightened, but she kept her temper and met him with a grace of her own. "I don't think you ought to ask me more questions than I ask you."

"Ah my dear," said the odd young man, "I'VE no mysteries. Why in the world, since it was what you came out for and have devoted so much of your time to, haven't you pulled

78

it off? Why haven't you married?"

"Why haven't YOU?" she retorted. "Do you think that if I had it would have been better for you?—that my husband would for a moment have put up with you? Do you mind my asking you if you'll kindly go NOW?" she went on after a glance at the clock. "I'm expecting a friend, whom I must see alone, on a matter of great importance—"

"And my being seen with you may compromise your respectability or undermine your nerve?" He sprawled imperturbably in his place, crossing again, in another sense, his long black legs and showing, above his low shoes, an absurd reach of parti–coloured sock. "I take your point well enough, but mayn't you be after all quite wrong? If you can't do anything for me couldn't you at least do something with me? If it comes to that, I'm clever and amusing and charming too! I've been such an ass that you don't appreciate me. But people like me—I assure you they do. They usually don't know what an ass I've been; they only see the surface, which"—and he stretched himself afresh as she looked him up and down—"you CAN imagine them, can't you, rather taken with? I'M 'what I am' too; nothing less and nothing more. That's true of us as a family, you see. We ARE a crew!" He delivered himself serenely. His voice was soft and flat, his pleasant eyes, his simple tones tending to the solemn, achieved at moments that effect of quaintness which is, in certain connexions, socially so known and enjoyed. "English people have quite a weakness for me—more than any others. I get on with them beautifully. I've always been with them abroad. They think me," the young man explained, "diabolically American."

"You!" Such stupidity drew from her a sigh of compassion.

Her companion apparently quite understood it. "Are you homesick, Mamie?" he asked, with wondering irrelevance.

The manner of the question made her, for some reason, in spite of her preoccupations, break into a laugh. A shade of indulgence, a sense of other things, came back to her. "You are funny, Scott!"

"Well," remarked Scott, "that's just what I claim. But ARE you so homesick?" he spaciously inquired, not as to a practical end, but from an easy play of intelligence.

"I'm just dying of it!" said Mamie Cutter.

"Why so am I!" Her visitor had a sweetness of concurrence.

"We're the only decent people," Miss Cutter declared. "And I know. You don't—you can't; and I can't explain. Come in," she continued with a return of her impatience and an increase of her decision, "at seven sharp."

She had quitted her seat some time before, and now, to get him into motion, hovered before him while, still motionless, he looked up at her. Something intimate, in the silence, appeared to pass between them—a community of fatigue and failure and, after all, of intelligence. There was a final cynical humour in it. It determined him, in any case, at last, and he slowly rose, taking in again as he stood there the testimony of the room. He might have been counting the photographs, but he looked at the flowers with detachment. "Who's coming?"

"Mrs. Medwin."

"American?"

"Dear no!"

"Then what are you doing for her?"

"I work for every one," she promptly returned.

"For every one who pays? So I suppose. Yet isn't it only we who do pay?"

There was a drollery, not lost on her, in the way his queer presence lent itself to his emphasised plural.

"Do you consider that YOU do?"

"At this, with his deliberation, he came back to his charming idea. "Only try me, and see if I can't be MADE to. Work me in." On her sharply presenting her back he stared a little at the clock. "If I come at seven may I stay to dinner?"

It brought her round again. "Impossible. I'm dining out."

80

"With whom?"

She had to think. "With Lord Considine."

"Oh my eye!" Scott exclaimed.

She looked at him gloomily. "Is THAT sort of tone what makes you pay? I think you might understand," she went on, "that if you're to sponge on me successfully you mustn't ruin me. I must have SOME remote resemblance to a lady."

"Yes? But why must _I_?" Her exasperated silence was full of answers, of which however his inimitable manner took no account. "You don't understand my real strength; I doubt if you even understand your own. You're clever, Mamie, but you're not so clever as I supposed. However," he pursued, "it's out of Mrs. Medwin that you'll get it."

"Get what?"

"Why the cheque that will enable you to assist me."

On this, for a moment, she met his eyes. "If you'll come back at seven sharp—not a minute before, and not a minute after, I'll give you two five–pound notes."

He thought it over. "Whom are you expecting a minute after?"

It sent her to the window with a groan almost of anguish, and she answered nothing till she had looked at the street. "If you injure me, you know, Scott, you'll be sorry."

"I wouldn't injure you for the world. What I want to do in fact is really to help you, and I promise you that I won't leave you—by which I mean won't leave London—till I've effected something really pleasant for you. I like you, Mamie, because I like pluck; I like you much more than you like me. I like you very, VERY much." He had at last with this reached the door and opened it, but he remained with his hand on the latch. "What does Mrs. Medwin want of you?" he thus brought out.

She had come round to see him disappear, and in the relief of this prospect she again just indulged him.

"The impossible."

He waited another minute. "And you're going to do it?"

"I'm going to do it," said Mamie Cutter.

"Well then that ought to be a haul. Call it THREE fivers!" he laughed. "At seven sharp." And at last he left her alone.

CHAPTER II

Miss Cutter waited till she heard the house–door close; after which, in a sightless mechanical way, she moved about the room readjusting various objects he had not touched. It was as if his mere voice and accent had spoiled her form. But she was not left too long to reckon with these things, for Mrs. Medwin was promptly announced. This lady was not, more than her hostess, in the first flush of her youth; her appearance—the scattered remains of beauty manipulated by taste—resembled one of the light repasts in which the fragments of yesterday's dinner figure with a conscious ease that makes up for the want of presence. She was perhaps of an effect still too immediate to be called interesting, but she was candid, gentle and surprised—not fatiguingly surprised, only just in the right degree; and her white face—it was too white—with the fixed eyes, the somewhat touzled hair and the Louis Seize hat, might at the end of the very long neck have suggested the head of a princess carried on a pike in a revolution. She immediately took up the business that had brought her, with the air however of drawing from the omens then discernible less confidence than she had hoped. The complication lay in the fact that if it was Mamie's part to present the omens, that lady yet had so to colour them as to make her own service large. She perhaps over–coloured; for her friend gave way to momentary despair.

"What you mean is then that it's simply impossible?"

"Oh no," said Mamie with a qualified emphasis. "It's POSSIBLE."

"But disgustingly difficult?"

Some Short Stories

"As difficult as you like."

"Then what can I do that I haven't done?"

"You can only wait a little longer."

"But that's just what I HAVE done. I've done nothing else. I'm always waiting a little longer!"

Miss Cutter retained, in spite of this pathos, her grasp of the subject. "THE thing, as I've told you, is for you first to be seen."

"But if people won't look at me?"

"They will."

"They WILL?" Mrs. Medwin was eager.

"They shall," her hostess went on. "It's their only having heard— without having seen.'"

"But if they stare straight the other way?" Mrs. Medwin continued to object. "You can't simply go up to them and twist their heads about."

"It's just what I can," said Mamie Cutter.

But her charming visitor, heedless for the moment of this attenuation, had found the way to put it. "It's the old story. You can't go into the water till you swim, and you can't swim till you go into the water. I can't be spoken to till I'm seen, but I can't be seen till I'm spoken to."

She met this lucidity, Miss Cutter, with but an instant's lapse. "You say I can't twist their heads about. But I HAVE twisted them."

It had been quietly produced, but it gave her companion a jerk. "They say 'Yes'?"

She summed it up. "All but one. SHE says 'No.'"

Mrs. Medwin thought; then jumped. "Lady Wantridge?"

Miss Cutter, as more delicate, only bowed admission. "I shall see her either this afternoon or late to–morrow. But she has written."

Her visitor wondered again. "May I see her letter?"

"No." She spoke with decision. "But I shall square her."

"Then how?"

"Well"—and Miss Cutter, as if looking upward for inspiration, fixed her eyes a while on the ceiling—"well, it will come to me."

Mrs. Medwin watched her—it was impressive. "And will they come to you—the others?" This question drew out the fact that they would– –so far at least as they consisted of Lady Edward, Lady Bellhouse and Mrs. Pouncer, who had engaged to muster, at the signal of tea, on the 14th—prepared, as it were, for the worst. There was of course always the chance that Lady Wantridge might take the field, in such force as to paralyse them, though that danger, at the same time, seemed inconsistent with her being squared. It didn't perhaps all quite ideally hang together; but what it sufficiently came to was that if she was the one who could do most FOR a person in Mrs. Medwin's position she was also the one who could do most against. It would therefore be distinctly what our friend familiarly spoke of as "collar–work." The effect of these mixed considerations was at any rate that Mamie eventually acquiesced in the idea, handsomely thrown out by her client, that she should have an "advance" to go on with. Miss Cutter confessed that it seemed at times as if one scarce COULD go on; but the advance was, in spite of this delicacy, still more delicately made—made in the form of a banknote, several sovereigns, some loose silver, and two coppers, the whole contents of her purse, neatly disposed by Mrs. Medwin on one of the tiny tables. It seemed to clear the air for deeper intimacies, the fruit of which was that Mamie, lonely after all in her crowd and always more helpful than helped, eventually brought out that the way Scott had been going on was what seemed momentarily to overshadow her own power to do so.

"I've had a descent from him." But she had to explain. "My half– brother—Scott Homer. A wretch."

84

"What kind of a wretch?"

"Every kind. I lose sight of him at times—he disappears abroad. But he always turns up again, worse than ever."

"Violent?"

"No."

"Maudlin?"

"No."

"Only unpleasant?"

"No. Rather pleasant. Awfully clever—awfully travelled and easy."

"Then what's the matter with him?"

Mamie mused, hesitated—seemed to see a wide past. "I don't know."

"Something in the background?" Then as her friend was silent, "Something queer about cards?" Mrs. Medwin threw off.

"I don't know—and I don't want to!"

"Ah well, I'm sure _I_ don't," Mrs. Medwin returned with spirit. The note of sharpness was perhaps also a little in the observation she made as she gathered herself to go. "Do you mind my saying something?"

Mamie took her eyes quickly from the money on the little stand. "You may say what you like."

"I only mean that anything awkward you may have to keep out of the way does seem to make more wonderful, doesn't it, that you should have got just where you are? I allude, you know, to your position."

"I see." Miss Cutter somewhat coldly smiled. "To my power."

"So awfully remarkable in an American."

"Ah you like us so."

Mrs. Medwin candidly considered. "But we don't, dearest."

Her companion's smile brightened. "Then why do you come to me?"

"Oh I like YOU!" Mrs. Medwin made out.

"Then that's it. There are no 'Americans.' It's always 'you.'"

"Me?" Mrs. Medwin looked lovely, but a little muddled.

"ME!" Mamie Cutter laughed. "But if you like me, you dear thing, you can judge if I like YOU." She gave her a kiss to dismiss her. "I'll see you again when I've seen her."

"Lady Wantridge? I hope so, indeed. I'll turn up late to—morrow, if you don't catch me first. Has it come to you yet?" the visitor, now at the door, went on.

"No; but it will. There's time."

"Oh a little less every day!"

Miss Cutter had approached the table and glanced again at the gold and silver and the note, not indeed absolutely overlooking the two coppers. "The balance," she put it, "the day after?"

"That very night if you like."

"Then count on me."

"Oh if I didn't—!" But the door closed on the dark idea. Yearningly then, and only when it had done so, Miss Cutter took up the money.

She went out with it ten minutes later, and, the calls on her time being many, remained out so long that at half—past six she hadn't come back. At that hour, on the other hand, Scott Homer knocked at her door, where her maid, who opened it with a weak pretence of holding it firm, ventured to announce to him, as a lesson well learnt, that he hadn't been expected till seven. No lesson, none the less, could prevail against his native art. He pleaded fatigue, her, the maid's, dreadful depressing London, and the need to curl up somewhere. If she'd just leave him quiet half an hour that old sofa upstairs would do for it; of which he took quickly such effectual possession that when five minutes later she peeped, nervous for her broken vow, into the drawing—room, the faithless young woman found him extended at his length and peacefully asleep.

CHAPTER III

The situation before Miss Cutter's return developed in other directions still, and when that event took place, at a few minutes past seven, these circumstances were, by the foot of the stair, between mistress and maid, the subject of some interrogative gasps and scared admissions. Lady Wantridge had arrived shortly after the interloper, and wishing, as she said, to wait, had gone straight up in spite of being told he was lying down.

"She distinctly understood he was there?"

"Oh yes ma'am; I thought it right to mention."

"And what did you call him?"

"Well, ma'am, I thought it unfair to YOU to call him anything but a gentleman."

Mamie took it all in, though there might well be more of it than one could quickly embrace. "But if she has had time," she flashed, "to find out he isn't one?"

"Oh ma'am, she had a quarter of an hour."

"Then she isn't with him still?"

"No ma'am; she came down again at last. She rang, and I saw her here, and she said she wouldn't wait longer."

Miss Cutter darkly mused. "Yet had already waited—?"

"Quite a quarter."

"Mercy on us!" She began to mount. Before reaching the top however she had reflected that quite a quarter was long if Lady Wantridge had only been shocked. On the other hand it was short if she had only been pleased. But how COULD she have been pleased? The very essence of their actual crisis was just that there was no pleasing her. Mamie had but to open the drawing—room door indeed to perceive that this was not true at least of Scott Homer, who was horribly cheerful.

Miss Cutter expressed to her brother without reserve her sense of the constitutional, the brutal selfishness that had determined his mistimed return. It had taken place, in violation of their agreement, exactly at the moment when it was most cruel to her that he should be there, and if she must now completely wash her hands of him he had only himself to thank. She had come in flushed with resentment and for a moment had been voluble, but it would have been striking that, though the way he received her might have seemed but to aggravate, it presently justified him by causing their relation really to take a stride. He had the art of confounding those who would quarrel with him by reducing them to the humiliation of a stirred curiosity.

"What COULD she have made of you?" Mamie demanded.

"My dear girl, she's not a woman who's eager to make too much of anything—anything, I mean, that will prevent her from doing as she likes, what she takes into her head. Of course," he continued to explain, "if it's something she doesn't want to do, she'll make as much as Moses."

Mamie wondered if that was the way he talked to her visitor, but felt obliged to own to his acuteness. It was an exact description of Lady Wantridge, and she was conscious of tucking it away for future use in a corner of her miscellaneous little mind. She withheld however all present acknowledgment, only addressing him another question. "Did you really get on with her?"

"Have you still to learn, darling—I can't help again putting it to you—that I get on with everybody? That's just what I don't seem able to drive into you. Only see how I get on with YOU."

She almost stood corrected. "What I mean is of course whether—"

"Whether she made love to me? Shyly, yet—or because—shamefully? She would certainly have liked awfully to stay."

"Then why didn't she?"

"Because, on account of some other matter—and I could see it was true—she hadn't time. Twenty minutes—she was here less—were all she came to give you. So don't be afraid I've frightened her away. She'll come back."

Mamie thought it over. "Yet you didn't go with her to the door?"

"She wouldn't let me, and I know when to do what I'm told—quite as much as what I'm not told. She wanted to find out about me. I mean from your little creature; a pearl of fidelity, by the way."

"But what on earth did she come up for?" Mamie again found herself appealing, and just by that fact showing her need of help.

"Because she always goes up." Then as, in the presence of this rapid generalisation, to say nothing of that of such a relative altogether, Miss Cutter could only show as comparatively blank: "I mean she knows when to go up and when to come down. She has instincts; she didn't know whom you might have up here. It's a kind of compliment to you anyway. Why Mamie," Scott pursued, "you don't know the curiosity we any of us inspire. You wouldn't believe what I've seen. The bigger bugs they are the more they're on the lookout."

Mamie still followed, but at a distance. "The lookout for what?"

"Why for anything that will help them to live. You've been here all this time without making out then, about them, what I've had to pick out as I can? They're dead, don't you see? And WE'RE alive."

"You? Oh!"—Mamie almost laughed about it.

"Well, they're a worn–out old lot anyhow; they've used up their resources. They do look out and I'll do them the justice to say they're not afraid—not even of me!" he continued as his sister again showed something of the same irony. "Lady Wantridge at any rate wasn't; that's what I mean by her having made love to me. She does what she likes. Mind it, you know." He was by this time fairly teaching her to read one of her best friends, and when, after it, he had come back to the great point of his lesson—that of her failure, through feminine inferiority, practically to grasp the truth that their being just as they were, he and she, was the real card for them to play—when he had renewed that reminder he left her absolutely in a state of dependence. Her impulse to press him on the subject of Lady Wantridge dropped; it was as if she had felt that, whatever had taken place, something would somehow come of it. She was to be in a manner disappointed, but the impression helped to keep her over to the next morning, when, as Scott had foretold, his new acquaintance did reappear, explaining to Miss Cutter that she had acted the day before to gain time and that she even now sought to gain it by not waiting longer. What, she promptly intimated she had asked herself, could that friend be thinking of? She must show where she stood before things had gone too far. If she had brought her answer without more delay she wished make it sharp. Mrs. Medwin? Never! "No, my dear—not I. THERE I stop."

Mamie had known it would be "collar–work," but somehow now, at the beginning she felt her heart sink. It was not that she had expected to carry the position with a rush, but that, as always after an interval, her visitor's defences really loomed—and quite, as it were, to the material vision—too large. She was always planted with them, voluminous, in the very centre of the passage; was like a person accommodated with a chair in some unlawful place at the theatre. She wouldn't move and you couldn't get round. Mamie's calculation indeed had not been on getting round; she was obliged to recognise that, too foolishly and fondly, she had dreamed of inducing a surrender. Her dream had been the fruit of her need; but, conscious that she was even yet unequipped for pressure, she felt, almost for the first time in her life, superficial and crude. She was to be paid—but with what was she, to that end, to pay? She had engaged to find an answer to this question, but the answer had not, according to her promise, "come." And Lady Wantridge meanwhile massed herself, and there was no view of her that didn't show her as verily, by some process too obscure to be traced, the hard depository of the social law. She was no younger, no fresher, no stronger, really, than any of them; she was only, with a kind of haggard fineness, a sharpened taste for life, and, with all sorts of things behind and beneath her, more abysmal and more immoral, more secure and more impertinent. The points she made were two in number. One was that she absolutely declined; the other was that she quite doubted if Mamie herself had measured the job. The thing couldn't be done. But say it COULD be; was Mamie quite the person to do it? To this Miss Cutter, with a sweet smile, replied that she quite understood how little she might seem so. "I'm only one of the persons to whom it has appeared that YOU are."

"Then who are the others?"

"Well, to begin with, Lady Edward, Lady Bellhouse and Mrs. Pouncer."

"Do you mean that they'll come to meet her?"

"I've seen them, and they've promised."

"To come, of course," Lady Wantridge said, "if _I_ come."

Her hostess cast about. "Oh of course you could prevent them. But I should take it as awfully kind of you not to. WON'T you do this for me?" Mamie pleaded.

Her friend looked over the room very much as Scott had done. "Do they really understand what it's FOR?"

"Perfectly. So that she may call."

"And what good will that do her?"

Miss Cutter faltered, but she presently brought it out. "Naturally what one hopes is that, you'll ask her."

"Ask her to call?"

"Ask her to dine. Ask her, if you'd be so truly sweet, for a Sunday; or something of that sort, and even if only in one of your MOST mixed parties, to Catchmore."

Miss Cutter felt the less hopeful after this effort in that her companion only showed a strange good nature. And it wasn't a satiric amiability, though it WAS amusement. "Take Mrs. Medwin into my family?"

"Some day when you're taking forty others."

"Ah but what I don't see is what it does for YOU. You're already so welcome among us that you can scarcely improve your position even by forming for us the most delightful relation."

"Well, I know how dear you are," Mamie Cutter replied; "but one has after all more than one side and more than one sympathy. I like her, you know." And even at this Lady Wantridge wasn't shocked; she showed that ease and blandness which were her way, unfortunately, of being most impossible. She remarked that SHE might listen to such things, because she was clever enough for them not to matter; only Mamie should take care how she went about saying them at large. When she became definite however, in a minute, on the subject of the public facts, Miss Cutter soon found herself ready to make her own concession. Of course she didn't dispute THEM: there they were; they were unfortunately on record, and, nothing was to be done about them but to—Mamie found it in truth at this point a little difficult.

"Well, what? Pretend already to have forgotten them?"

"Why not, when you've done it in so many other cases?"

"There ARE no other cases so bad. One meets them at any rate as they come. Some you can manage, others you can't. It's no use, you must give them up. They're past patching; there's nothing to be done with them. There's nothing accordingly to be done with Mrs. Medwin but to put her off." And Lady Wantridge rose to her height.

"Well, you know, I DO do things," Mamie quavered with a smile so strained that it partook of exaltation.

"You help people? Oh yes, I've known you to do wonders. But stick," said Lady Wantridge with strong and cheerful emphasis, "to your Americans!"

Miss Cutter, gazing, got up. "You don't do justice, Lady Wantridge, to your own compatriots. Some of them are really charming. Besides," said Mamie, "working for mine often strikes me, so far as the interest—the inspiration and excitement, don't you know?—go, as rather too easy. You all, as I constantly have occasion to say, like us so!"

Her companion frankly weighed it. "Yes; it takes that to account for your position. I've always thought of you nevertheless as keeping for their benefit a regular working agency. They come to you, and you place them. There remains, I confess," her ladyship went on in the same free spirit, "the great wonder—"

"Of how I first placed my poor little self? Yes," Mamie bravely conceded, "when _I_ began there was no agency. I just worked my passage. I didn't even come to YOU, did I? You never noticed me till, as Mrs. Short Stokes says, 'I was 'way, 'way up!' Mrs. Medwin," she threw in, "can't get over it." Then, as her friend looked vague: "Over my social situation."

"Well, it's no great flattery to you to say," Lady Wantridge good– humouredly returned, "that she certainly can't hope for one resembling it." Yet it really seemed to spread there before them. "You simply MADE Mrs. Short Stokes."

"In spite of her name!" Mamie smiled.

"Oh your 'names'—! In spite of everything."

"Ah I'm something of an artist." With which, and a relapse marked by her wistful eyes into the gravity of the matter, she supremely fixed her friend. She felt how little she minded betraying at last the extremity of her need, and it was out of this extremity that her appeal proceeded. "Have I really had your last word? It means so much to me."

Lady Wantridge came straight to the point. "You mean you depend on it?"

"Awfully!"

"Is it all you have?"

"All. Now."

"But Mrs. Short Stokes and the others—'rolling,' aren't they? Don't they pay up?"

"Ah," sighed Mamie, "if it wasn't for THEM—!"

Lady Wantridge perceived. "You've had so much?"

"I couldn't have gone on."

"Then what do you do with it all?"

"Oh most of it goes back to them. There are all sorts, and it's all help. Some of them have nothing."

"Oh if you feed the hungry," Lady Wantridge laughed, "you're indeed in a great way of business. Is Mrs. Medwin"—her transition was immediate—"really rich?"

"Really. He left her everything."

"So that if I do say 'yes'—"

"It will quite set me up."

"I see—and how much more responsible it makes one! But I'd rather myself give you the money."

"Oh!" Mamie coldly murmured.

"You mean I mayn't suspect your prices? Well, I daresay I don't! But I'd rather give you ten pounds."

"Oh!" Mamie repeated in a tone that sufficiently covered her prices. The question was in every way larger. "Do you never forgive?" she reproachfully inquired. The door opened however at the moment she spoke and Scott Homer presented himself.

CHAPTER IV

Scott Homer wore exactly, to his sister's eyes, the aspect he had worn the day before, and it also formed to her sense the great feature of his impartial greeting.

"How d'ye do, Mamie? How d'ye do, Lady Wantridge?"

"How d'ye do again?" Lady Wantridge replied with an equanimity striking to her hostess. It was as if Scott's own had been contagious; it was almost indeed as if she had seen him before. Had she ever so seen him—before the previous day? While Miss Cutter put to herself this question her visitor at all events met the one she had previously uttered. "Ever 'forgive'?" this personage echoed in a tone that made as little account as possible of the interruption. "Dear yes! The people I HAVE forgiven!" She laughed—perhaps a little nervously; and she was now looking at Scott. The way she looked at him was precisely what had already had its effect for his sister. "The people I can!"

"Can you forgive me?" asked Scott Homer.

She took it so easily. "But—what?"

Mamie interposed; she turned directly to her brother. "Don't try her. Leave it so." She had had an inspiration, it was the most extraordinary thing in the world. "Don't try HIM"—she had turned to their companion. She looked grave, sad, strange. "Leave it so." Yes, it was a distinct inspiration, which she couldn't have explained, but which had come, prompted by something she had caught—the extent of the recognition expressed—in Lady Wantridge's face. It had come absolutely of a sudden, straight out of the opposition of the two figures before her—quite as if a concussion had struck a light. The light was helped by her quickened sense that her friend's silence on the incident of the day before showed some sort of consciousness. She looked surprised. "Do you know my brother?"

"DO I know you?" Lady Wantridge asked of him.

"No, Lady Wantridge," Scott pleasantly confessed, "not one little mite!"

"Well then if you MUST go—" and Mamie offered her a hand. "But I'll go down with you. NOT YOU!" she launched at her brother, who immediately effaced himself. His way of doing so—and he had already done so, as for Lady Wantridge, in respect to their previous encounter—struck her even at the moment as an instinctive if slightly blind tribute to her possession of an idea; and as such, in its celerity, made her so admire him, and their common wit, that she on the spot more than forgave him his queerness. He was right. He could be as queer as he liked! The queerer the better! It was at the foot of the stairs, when she had got her guest down, that what she had assured Mrs. Medwin would come did indeed come. "DID you meet him here yesterday?"

"Dear yes. Isn't he too funny?"

"Yes," said Mamie gloomily. "He IS funny. But had you ever met him before?"

"Dear no!"

"Oh!"—and Mamie's tone might have meant many things.

Lady Wantridge however, after all, easily overlooked it. "I only knew he was one of your odd Americans. That's why, when I heard yesterday here that he was up there awaiting your return, I didn't let that prevent me. I thought he might be. He certainly," her ladyship laughed, "IS."

"Yes, he's very American," Mamie went on in the same way.

"As you say, we ARE fond of you! Good–bye," said Lady Wantridge.

But Mamie had not half done with her. She felt more and more—or she hoped at least—that she looked strange. She WAS, no doubt, if it came to that, strange. "Lady Wantridge," she almost convulsively broke out, "I don't know whether you'll understand me, but I seem to feel that I must act with you—I don't know what to call it!—responsibly. He IS my brother."

"Surely—and why not?" Lady Wantridge stared. "He's the image of you!"

"Thank you!"—and Mamie was stranger than ever.

"Oh he's good–looking. He's handsome, my dear. Oddly—but distinctly!" Her ladyship was for treating it much as a joke.

But Mamie, all sombre, would have none of this. She boldly gave him up. "I think he's awful."

"He is indeed—delightfully. And where DO you get your ways of saying things? It isn't anything—and the things aren't anything. But it's so droll."

"Don't let yourself, all the same," Mamie consistently pursued, "be carried away by it. The thing can't be done—simply."

Lady Wantridge wondered. "'Done simply'?"

"Done at all."

"But what can't be?"

"Why, what you might think—from his pleasantness. What he spoke of your doing for him."

Lady Wantridge recalled. "Forgiving him?"

"He asked you if you couldn't. But you can't. It's too dreadful for me, as so near a relation, to have, loyally—loyally to YOU—to say it. But he's impossible."

It was so portentously produced that her ladyship had somehow to meet it. "What's the matter with him?"

"I don't know."

"Then what's the matter with YOU?" Lady Wantridge inquired.

"It's because I WON'T know," Mamie—not without dignity—explained.

"Then _I_ won't either."

"Precisely. Don't. It's something," Mamie pursued, with some inconsequence, "that—somewhere or other, at some time or other—he appears to have done. Something that has made a difference in his life."

"'Something'?" Lady Wantridge echoed again. "What kind of thing?"

Mamie looked up at the light above the door, through which the London sky was doubly dim. "I haven't the least idea."

"Then what kind of difference?"

Mamie's gaze was still at the light. "The difference you see."

Lady Wantridge, rather obligingly, seemed to ask herself what she saw. "But I don't see any! It seems, at least," she added, "such an amusing one! And he has such nice eyes."

"Oh DEAR eyes!" Mamie conceded; but with too much sadness, for the moment, about the connexions of the subject, to say more.

It almost forced her companion after an instant to proceed. "Do you mean he can't go home?"

She weighed her responsibility. "I only make out—more's the pity!—that he doesn't."

"Is it then something too terrible—?"

She thought again. "I don't know what—for men—IS too terrible."

"Well then as you don't know what 'is' for women either—good–bye!" her visitor laughed.

It practically wound up the interview; which, however, terminating thus on a considerable stir of the air, was to give Miss Cutter for several days the sense of being much blown about. The degree to which, to begin with, she had been drawn—or perhaps rather pushed– –closer to Scott was marked in the brief colloquy that she on her friend's departure had with him. He had immediately said it. "You'll see if she doesn't ask me down!"

"So soon?"

"Oh I've known them at places—at Cannes, at Pau, at Shanghai—do it sooner still. I always know when they will. You CAN'T make out they don't love me!" He spoke almost plaintively, as if he wished she could.

"Then I don't see why it hasn't done you more good."

"Why Mamie," he patiently reasoned, "what more good COULD it? As I tell you," he explained, "it has just been my life."

"Then why do you come to me for money?"

"Oh they don't give me THAT!" Scott returned.

"So that it only means then, after all, that I, at the best, must keep you up?"

He fixed on her the nice eyes Lady Wantridge admired. "Do you mean to tell me that already—at this very moment—I'm not distinctly keeping you?"

She gave him back his look. "Wait till she HAS asked you, and then," Mamie added, "decline."

Scott, not too grossly, wondered. "As acting for YOU?"

Mamie's next injunction was answer enough. "But BEFORE—yes— call."

He took it in. "Call—but decline. Good!"

"The rest," she said, "I leave to you." And she left it in fact with such confidence that for a couple of days she was not only conscious of no need to give Mrs. Medwin another turn of the screw, but positively evaded, in her fortitude, the reappearance of that lady. It was not till the fourth day that she waited upon her, finding her, as she had expected, tense.

"Lady Wantridge WILL—?"

"Yes, though she says she won't."

"She says she won't? O—oh!" Mrs. Medwin moaned.

"Sit tight all the same. I HAVE her!"

"But how?"

"Through Scott—whom she wants."

"Your bad brother!" Mrs. Medwin stared. "What does she want of him?"

"To amuse them at Catchmore. Anything for that. And he WOULD. But he shan't!" Mamie declared. "He shan't go unless she comes. She must meet you first—you're my condition."

"O—o—oh!" Mrs. Medwin's tone was a wonder of hope and fear. "But doesn't he want to go?"

"He wants what I want. She draws the line at YOU. I draw the line at HIM."

"But SHE—doesn't she mind that he's bad?"

It was so artless that Mamie laughed. "No—it doesn't touch her. Besides, perhaps he isn't. It isn't as for you—people seem not to know. He has settled everything, at all events, by going to see her. It's before her that he's the thing she'll have to have."

"Have to?"

"For Sundays in the country. A feature—THE feature."

"So she has asked him?"

"Yes—and he has declined."

"For ME?" Mrs. Medwin panted.

"For me," said Mamie on the door–step. "But I don't leave him for long." Her hansom had waited. "She'll come."

Lady Wantridge did come. She met in South Audley Street, on the fourteenth, at tea, the ladies whom Mamie had named to her, together with three or four others, and it was rather a master– stroke for Miss Cutter that if Mrs. Medwin was modestly present Scott Homer was as markedly not. This occasion, however, is a medal that would take rare casting, as would also, for that matter, even the minor light and shade, the lower relief, of the pecuniary transaction that Mrs. Medwin's flushed gratitude scarce awaited the dispersal of the company munificently to complete. A new understanding indeed on the spot rebounded from it, the conception of which, in Mamie's mind, had promptly bloomed. "He shan't go now unless he takes you." Then, as her fancy always moved quicker for her client than her client's own—"Down with him to Catchmore! When he goes to amuse them YOU," she serenely developed, "shall amuse them too." Mrs. Medwin's response was again rather oddly divided, but she was sufficiently intelligible when it came to meeting the hint that this latter provision would represent success to the tune of a separate fee. "Say," Mamie had suggested, "the same."

"Very well; the same."

The knowledge that it was to be the same had perhaps something to do also with the obliging spirit in which Scott eventually went. It was all at the last rather hurried—a party rapidly got together for the Grand Duke, who was in England but for the hour, who had good–naturedly proposed himself, and who liked his parties small, intimate and funny. This one was of the smallest and was finally judged to conform neither too little nor too much to the other conditions—after a brief whirlwind of wires and counterwires, and an iterated waiting of hansoms at various doors—to include Mrs. Medwin. It was from Catchmore itself that, snatching, a moment—on the wondrous Sunday afternoon, this lady had the harmonious thought of sending the new cheque. She was in bliss enough, but her scribble none the less intimated that it was Scott who amused them most. He WAS the feature.

Printed in the United Kingdom
by Lightning Source UK Ltd.
104665UKS00002BA/12